It's in His Bite

Jillian Rink

*For Everyone**

**Those who also had daydreams about a British vampire
professor making you feel all kinds of ways*

Chapter One

Harlowe

The vampire in the corner of the mountain coffee shop was doing a shit job of hiding his hunger. I palmed the disposable cup and lifted it to my lips, letting the warmth of the black tea fill my lungs, not quite ready to risk burning my tongue. The vampire's gaze flitted across the moderate crowd, his cheeks hollowing out as the seconds ticked by. He ran a hand over his mouth, his eyes closing as he swallowed. Another couple minutes, and he'd probably break down and try his luck with one of the unwitting patrons of this little place tucked deep in the Rocky Mountains.

It was easy enough to imagine how the scene would play out. He'd abandon the half-drunk coffee that was his excuse to be here and casually tap a shoulder—or maybe a wrist or back of hand. Only a quick brush would be needed, a moment of his skin on theirs. The unsuspecting human would heed the unspoken command, following him to his car or the side of the building, where he would be able to slake his thirst without risking exposure. Another quick touch, and all memory of the experience would be gone, scrubbed from the person's memory.

Yes, imagining it was as simple as envisioning what I might wear tomorrow. I had seen Tessa, my best friend, do it countless times, the sequence so fine-tuned it was nearly ethereal to witness. She, though, never let the need reach a point where it was so plainly visible on her face. It wasn't safe.

I eyed the one in the corner with pursed lips. It was irresponsible in the extreme for him to have let it get to this point. One camera turned in the wrong direction, and there'd be mass hysteria all over social media. Even as I watched, his eyes flashed red then back to brown.

Foolish, reckless vampire.

Vampires weren't known by the general populace, just like the rest of the preternaturals that melded and blended well enough. The wolves tended to band together in rural towns where it was easier to run uninhibited. There was a group here, though none had ventured inside this coffee shop yet today. Witches were often wanderers, moving from one place to another, a seemingly inescapable urge to keep discovering, to keep seeking, running through their veins. That's how my mother described it, at least.

But vampires were truly the ones that adored cities, the large swaths of people and metal and commotion. They drank it in nearly as fiercely as the blood they needed to survive. Most wouldn't be found this deep into the mountains without a damn good reason, like those coming in the next few days to my parents' cabin a few miles outside this little town to celebrate Christmas.

Curiosity burned through me, but I squashed it down. It was a gift from my mother, just like the wanderlust. My father's gifts were more obvious, my red hair and brown eyes and impish nose. Unlike my brother, I didn't end up with fangs or the need for blood. Dhampirs are like that, though. Genetics are weird.

While my brother looked like my mother and embodied my father, I was the opposite. Even now, graduated from college for nearly six months and newly turned 22, I felt unmoored. Sure, I'd applied for an internship with an archeology nonprofit on the Iberian peninsula. It was why I waited in this charming shop rather than continue on to the cabin, unwilling to be alone when the email of whether I got the position came today. My best friends wouldn't be here until later this evening, and there was simply no way I'd be able to ignore the email for that long.

My mother had offered a place in her business after I graduated, something that would keep me closer to home after spending the last four years in another state. It would let me use my own magic in the same tradition as all the women in her family, but the idea chafed, set my teeth on edge. There was just something... missing. I wasn't sold on the idea that this internship was it, but it sparked enough interest to keep me from quietly spiraling into boredom.

The vampire took a long swig of his drink and then rolled his shoulders. After a minute, his body grew tense, like a predator preparing to strike. He'd decided which human to try and enthrall. His hands clenched the cup, and his fingers extended into sharp claws. His eyes flashed red again, taking several seconds to flick back to the rich brown.

There was no possible way this would end well for the human. Which meant it would end poorly for the vampire, as well. The last thing any preternatural wanted was to end up in the crosshairs of the Enforcers, witches specially trained to clean up after all of us and keep us hidden. Their methods were... brutal. And while it was often impossible to tell exactly how old a vampire was—they could live for centuries, after all—there was something about *this* one that screamed inexperienced. I'd bet my collection of vintage vinyl records he was turned, not born, and probably only in the last few years.

Something almost like sympathy twisted in my gut.

Damn it.

I risked a drink of my London fog, letting the warmth trace under my sternum like liquid courage. And then I tilted my head, exposing the delicate, tender flesh of my throat in an invitation the vampire would understand even across the room. His eyes flashed red as his gaze locked on the column of untouched skin. His lip pulled back, revealing a flash of his fang. My thighs clenched in primal anticipation.

Despite the bite being something pleasurable, not all feedings ended with sex. But the way this vampire was eyeing my offered carotid? It seemed likely I'd end up getting an orgasm in exchange for my blood. A worthy trade, and the only time I willingly offered my vein.

He rose from the table, more leashed violence than unearthly grace—like he was a werewolf rather than a blood drinker—and stalked toward me. I took a long pull of my drink, letting my eyes close as he neared. His voice was surprisingly high as he whispered in my ear.

"Yours or mine, witch?"

I bristled under the label. Dhampirs were *not* witches, just like they were not human nor vampire. We were a half-breed, granted gifts from both our parents, each of us wholly unique.

"Yours." I didn't dare risk my father smelling an unknown vampire in my car. It wouldn't be worth the inevitable argument. "And it's dhampir, not witch."

His breath caught, and I could practically feel him vibrating with new excitement. Vampires needed blood to survive, just as the wolves needed the moon to unleash their beast and witches needed the earth to align their magics. And just like how the witches were able to take from the earth for extra power when needed, vampires could take into themselves the magic of those they fed from. It's why vampires only ever shared their blood with a chosen mate or their creations. My blood? It would give him more than any of the humans here could ever dream of supplying.

"Let's go," he whispered.

Without a word, I grabbed my bag and followed him out onto the main street of the small mountain town. Large, fluffy snowflakes fell around us, already sticking to the slick concrete as he led me to a newer SUV parked along a side alley. He all but vibrated with his need now that we weren't under such close scrutiny. Even still, he opened the back door carefully and gestured me inside first before silently following. The door clicked closed. I set my drink in the cup holder and twisted my hair off my neck, not wanting to risk getting it bloody. He waited with an unnerving focus, his hands elongated into those claws again. His eyes had stopped switching back and forth. Now just the eerie red of his need shone.

Not bothering to fill the silence, I tilted my neck in the same gesture as before. His teeth were a slash of pain before there was nothing but pleasure.

Chapter Two

Harlowe

Just my luck, there was already another car in front of the cabin by the time I pulled up to it a few hours later. It wasn't my parents, so at least there was one small mercy mixed in with my idiotic choice to help that vampire. I dug through my bag the moment I parked, trying to find the aftercare ointment for the bite. I'd been right: he hadn't been gentle. If I'd been human, there would have been no way to hide the damage he'd done. As it was, the marks were puffy at the edges, and the scabs were barely set—any significant twist of my neck and they would break back open, just like they had when he'd guided my knees around his hips and fucked me.

I twisted off the lid to the ointment and carefully dabbed it onto the marks, resisting the urge to sink my nails into the skin. It was already itchy enough I wanted to rip my skin clean off. That didn't bode well for the rest of tonight and tomorrow.

"Damn it, Harlowe," I muttered. The ointment stung where I applied it, and I hissed through my teeth. "Next time, just let the poor fool get in trouble. The orgasm wasn't even worth it."

Not anywhere near worth it, if I was being completely honest with myself. The last time I'd been with a man that clueless about my clit, I'd been a teen, and we'd both been virgins.

A drop of blood slowly trailed down my neck. I heaved a sigh and got out of the car, grabbing my bag with an aggravation I rarely felt. Hopefully Mom's ready-for-anything first aid kit was still prepped up here because these were going to need more than a careless swipe of the vampire's tongue and the anti-itch cream I always kept on me.

The walkway was already covered in a fresh layer of powder, the snow falling heavier than even an hour before. That snowstorm had settled over the immediate mountain range just like the meteorologists suggested it might. A flicker of unease twisted my stomach. Hopefully Tessa and Rhiannon had managed to start their way over the pass earlier than they'd originally planned. Driving the pass at night was already not all that great, and add in the heavy snow? Absolutely not something I wanted either of them trying.

I stomped off my shoes and then hurried to the kitchen, dumping my bag and jacket on the counter without any kind of decorum. The itching was getting even worse, burrowing so deep it felt like it might become permanent. I couldn't help but scratch at it. One of the scabs ripped open, and I hissed, grabbing the hand towel and pressing it to the punctures. Getting blood on this sweater would just be the icing on the metaphorical cake that was this morning.

Damn it, this was why I didn't offer my vein to vampires. For humans, their bite was innocuous. As long as the vampire took the time to close the wounds with their saliva, not even a pinprick of a scab was left behind. They didn't itch, didn't bruise. But for all of us supernaturals? Even the most gentle bite left behind wounds that scabbed and bruised and itched like the world's worst mosquito bite on steroids.

The door to the deck opened and then closed, letting in a sudden gust of cold air that sent a shiver down my spine.

"Harlowe?" The rich caramel voice held an unwavering authority, but it wasn't the thread of dominance that had my heart racing between one moment and the next. No, it was the distinct, posh British accent that curled around the vowels of my name like a damn drug. "Why do I smell blood?"

My breathing froze as my body locked down.

Fuck my life.

Turned out, there was actually no mercy from the universe today. My parents might not be here yet, but Landon Rhodes was nearly as bad. Of all of my parents' friends that would be here in the next few days to celebrate Christmas, *this* one was the worst possible option. It wasn't just that he'd been best friends with my dad for years, though he'd only moved from London and joined our clan a little over a year ago. Not even the fact he was stoic and acerbic in every group interaction I'd ever witnessed, and all of my brother's friends had multiple stories of his ruthless adherence to not only the secrecy law but the clan-specific code of ethics around finding blood hosts. Or that he'd been responsible for more than one idiotic teenager getting in a world of trouble with the clan leadership.

No, the worst part was that despite understanding exactly how asinine it was, my heart raced any time I was near him. My stomach twisted with butterflies and my cheeks flushed a bright red every time his eyes locked with mine. The worst part was that I had an impossible crush on my father's best friend.

The universe truly hated me. Why else would he be the one to find me with a vampire's poorly tended bite in the side of my throat and the scent of sex clinging to my clothes? This was worse than any walk of shame I'd done in college.

I tried to ignore his steps as they echoed through the large great room, opening the cabinet above the sink and pulling the sunflower-decorated bin that held enough wound care products to practically qualify as an urgent care. Blood seeped through the hand towel, so I twisted the fabric and used more pressure.

"Did you cut yourself?" Landon asked, true worry now laced through his voice.

I didn't answer, ignoring the flush of my cheeks as I pulled one of the large pieces of gauze from the bin and tried to rip it open. The footfalls came faster, and then a gentle, warm hand was pulling the towel away from my neck, his hold featherlight where his fingers brushed my palm. Just the slight touch had his voice suddenly filling my mind.

Who in the hell did she let bite her? Joshua's going to be—

I sucked in a gasp and quickly twisted my hand out of his hold, cutting off the flow of his thoughts. It was my unique ability, the odd manifestation of my hybrid genetics. I could hear the thoughts of anyone I touched, my palm to their skin. It was invasive and jarring, something I'd never gotten used to. It was also a secret. Only a handful of people knew, and Landon wasn't one of them.

Landon frowned but said nothing, all of his attention returning to my neck. He moved the towel fully away from my skin.

"Bloody hell." His curse was vehement for all that it was a whisper. "What idiotic fool doesn't make sure his bite is closed before leaving?"

He dropped the towel as if it burned him and then grabbed the thicker gauze from the bin, dabbing it against the bite before cursing again. A muscle feathered in his jaw while he pulled supplies from the bin, everything I'd meant to grab before he barged in. Gauze and bandages. Mom's clotting tonic. The larger of two jars of her anti-itch cream, too.

"It's not like this is the first time I've been a blood host." My cheeks flushed darker. I pulled the clotting tonic from his grasp and unscrewed the lid. "I can take care of it."

"The bastard bit too deep." He scowled, his eyes flashing red, and ripped open a new bandage. "You've bled through a towel and an entire packet of gauze. Like hell can you take care of it."

I rolled my eyes.

Was this bite bad? Yes. Had I had others similar? Unfortunately, also yes. Aftercare sucked when they were this messy, but I wasn't a bumbling idiot about it all.

I carefully tipped the tonic's bottle, letting five drops fall into my palm, quietly praying it was the fast-acting version of

Mom's recipe. Each dot stilled against my skin and then slowly expanded into the white foam I needed.

Landon stood close enough I could feel the heat of his body, could smell the snow and pine forest on the gray sweater he wore, could see the small gray hairs at his temple and peppered through his close-trim beard. Those butterflies I always had around him swarmed in my stomach and made it hard to breathe. I needed to get him away from me before I said something truly stupid.

"You don't need to stand here and snarl at me like you're my dad," I groused as I pulled the gauze away and pressed my palm of tonic to the bites.

His green eyes narrowed and then flashed red a second time.

"If you don't want me to tell your father, you will stop talking while I bandage it," he muttered.

I narrowed my eyes. "You wouldn't."

He raised a single eyebrow, the same way I'd seen him do countless times when dealing with an irritating vampire at one of the clan functions. "You bet your arse I will. Now shut up while I keep you from bleeding all over the kitchen."

Chapter Three

Harlowe

Having Landon Rhodes anywhere in the same room as me was an exquisite agony borne of idiotic attraction, but having him herd me to the kitchen island and then crowd me into the barstool while he was no more than an inch away from my body? It was worse. I was close enough to smell the dark, musky cologne he wore and see the subtle muscles that filled out his sweater and slacks.

Slacks. Like this was some damn class at the university and not my parents' annual Christmas retreat.

His eyes were bright green jewels as he worked to clean up the bites. Every so often, they would flash that ominous red that had my breath catching in my throat. And every time, his jaw would clench and a muscle would feather in his neck.

His hands were soft but unrelenting, and each brush of his skin against the sensitive wounds had a shiver coasting down my spine and an ache ratcheting deeper in my belly. When he twisted to grab the adhesive bandage, his knee brushed my own, and I practically collapsed in a puddle on the floor. It took every ounce of self-preservation to keep the whimper buried deep enough he wouldn't hear it.

Holy sex appeal.

Sure, I was attracted to men, but all of my most memorable partners were women. They just... Well, they never once left their bites half-bleeding when kicking me out of the back of their SUV after not delivering a single damn orgasm, that's for sure. God, the bar was literally in hell and some guys couldn't manage to get above it.

So how did this man manage to make me *this* high strung without uttering a damn word outside of threatening to tell my father I let a random vampire feed from me? Truly, the universe held no good will for me. This was the worst torture I'd ever had to endure.

"You need to check this tonight. If it's broken open, you'll need another treatment of Meridith's wound tonic," he said into the overbearing silence.

The sudden rumble of his voice made me start. He frowned, taking me in with a look that seemed to dig right through me. God, I hoped I didn't look as flustered as I felt.

After a long beat, he continued. "I don't trust that it will stay closed. The wanker did a piss poor job of handling his marks."

I forced a swallow and then nodded, ready to slide off this stool and hide in the large bedroom I'd share with all of the single women on their way while obsessively refreshing my email like I'd been doing at the cafe. I carefully got to my feet and reached for my bag, trying to not hit Landon as he took a step back.

Except he didn't move. He stood utterly still, a wall of muscle and wool and old money charisma, his eyes flashing back to the bite and away in a circuit.

Why had he not backed away? Was he waiting for me to say something? Because there was absolutely no way I was going to be able to talk when he was so damn close to me. I wasn't even sure words could form at this point.

That muscle ticked in his neck again, and his eyes skated over my face. His eyes glowed that eerie red for an entire minute before fading back to green. I couldn't help but focus on his lips, the way they were a pale pink and way too full for his face, the way the soft lines of them smoothed the harder cut of his chin and the rugged feel of his beard.

The ringing of my phone had me practically jumping out of my skin. He finally took that step away, twisting to grab all the wound supplies from the counter.

Rhiannon's face filled the screen as I answered the call. Her blonde hair was pulled back, only the blunt bangs framing her face. Her gaze was on something behind the phone. Heavy steps sounded through the speaker and then a low growl that was distinctly wolf-like.

"For God's sake," Rhiannon said, her hold on the phone twisting so that I could see more of her parents' living room. "Dylan, would you just go for a run and save us the misery of being stuck going over the pass with you like this?"

The growling got louder before it cut off all at once.

"Go," a different feminine voice ordered. I was almost

positive it was Rhiannon and Dylan's mother, Ferne. "You have half an hour before we're leaving. Get yourself sorted."

"Rhiannon?" I asked in a dry tone.

Her attention snapped back to me, a light pink blush coloring her cheeks.

"Oh, hey, Harlowe! Just wanted to let you know that—" Her eyes locked on the bandage. "What happened?"

I rolled my eyes. "Nothing."

Landon scoffed.

"You have a bandage," Rhiannon said with a frown. "That's not nothing."

"Bandage?" Tessa appeared in the frame. Her chocolate brown hair was down, and she'd decided to wear it in its natural ringlets. Her olive skin was glowing against the cream sweater she wore.

She and Rhiannon were polar opposites—not just in looks but in personality, too. Rhiannon was exuberant and rash where Tessa was restrained ferocity and pragmatism. And, just like my red hair was a sort-of middle ground between their blonde and brown, my whimsy and temperance was the third side of the triangle that balanced our friendship.

Tessa's eyes sharpened as she saw the bandage on my neck, too.

"What happened?"

I took a step away from the kitchen and waved off her concern. "Nothing. Just blood hosted."

Landon snorted. "Ah, yes, because the typical blood host has to use specialty wound tonic to keep from bleeding out on the kitchen island."

Tessa and Rhiannon both froze for thirty long seconds.

And then Rhiannon's face changed, an excitement in them that wasn't there before. She grabbed Tessa's arm, and then the scene around them was changing as she took them somewhere alone.

The moment she stopped moving, she asked, "Wait, did you—"

My cheeks flushed so fast I could feel my chest and neck warm, too. I swore to God, if she spilled my most damnable secret, I would literally die. Just let me melt into the floor now because there was no way I would be able to come back from that.

My reply was too sharp. "No!"

Landon glanced up, a single eyebrow raised. It felt like he was digging too deep again. My cheeks were so dark, they alone were probably betraying my crush.

Tessa pointedly cleared her throat.

"Rhiannon was just calling to let you know we're all heading up together in another hour or so. We should be there a bit before dinner as long as they don't close the pass."

"Great," I managed to say.

But I couldn't tear my gaze away from Landon as he dumped the wound care into the trash, washed his hands, and reorganized the bin of supplies. His movements were smooth and precise but with a coiled power I'd seen radiate off of nearly every vampire I'd ever met at some point. It wasn't much of a surprise that my bleeding had set off his own hunger.

Not muttering another word and without bothering to grab a coat, he opened the door and stepped onto the deck. He hopped over the railing, dropping out of sight. My breath caught, the rational part of my brain freaking out over the two-story fall despite understanding that all of us preternaturals were stronger, faster, and more capable than the humans around us.

"Have you gotten the email yet?" Rhiannon asked.

I forced myself to breathe deeply, trying to rationalize it was just to calm myself down, to recenter myself after... all of that. But most of me just wanted one more chance to smell the musk and citrus blend that was uniquely Landon.

"Um, no, not yet," I said. "Part of me thinks it won't come until tomorrow."

"Dang it." Rhiannon's curse was vehement.

"So you're going to tell us what actually happened now, right?" Tessa asked, her voice sly. "Because we need to know why Landon fucking Rhodes was just cleaning up your neck, Harlowe. Now."

With a breathless giggle, I pressed my bag against my belly and tucked into the window seat at the top of the stairs, happy enough to let my friends distract me.

Chapter Four

Landon

I ran, moving fast enough to not be seen by the humans that were in the scattered homes and cabins along the winding road, and did not dare slow for one second. The air was bitterly cold against my skin, but it didn't touch the heat racing through my veins. My hands were thrumming with the entirely asinine desire to feel the smooth silk of her skin again. The need to turn around was almost too intense to ignore. The subtle fragrance of her shampoo or lotion—gods, it could even be a perfume—was imprinted in my mind, the fruity undertones and the stronger vanilla. I gritted my teeth and ignored the dual aches of my fangs and dick, forcing more distance between me and that kitchen.

Snow fell all around me, so thick it was nearly impossible to see through. The sharpened vision brought by my transformed gaze rendered every individual flake in irritating detail as if *they* were suitable options for slaking my hunger.

Hunger that had been reasonably handled early this morning before getting to the Grants' mountain cabin just before lunch.

Sure, smelling a person's blood could heighten a vampire's hunger, and there had been enough of hers to act as prop to a thriller movie. It certainly had impacted me. Except it wasn't just her blood that had my body growing thirstier with every passing second. Or even mostly. It was seeing the bite and smelling the other vampire all over her. It was, for one bare instant, the image of his fangs in her throat while she moaned under him. It was the way her breath shuddered with every swipe of the gauze like the bite was still giving her pleasure—which was something that could happen, though it wasn't very common.

No, my eyes were sharpened and my fangs were pressing into my bottom gums because all I could see when that towel moved was the instant lewd daydream that they had been my fangs and hands and tongue that had marked her, touched her, caressed her.

Bloody hell, my body should not be thrumming with this kind of want. Not for Harlowe. Not for my best friend's *daughter*. I'd held her as an infant, for fuck's sake, before Joshua and Meridith had returned to her family's coven in America.

None of that seemed to matter to my body, though. It hadn't stopped being this agonizing mass of twisted desire since Joshua had reintroduced us at a clan function last summer. Her bright red hair had been curled and pulled away from her face, leaving it to cascade down her back. Her heart-shaped face was lean, the column of her throat graceful. Her subtle curves and toned legs were a man's fantasy.

And the sparkle in her eye, like she knew a secret and just couldn't wait for you to discover exactly what it was? All of it was a far cry from the awkward twelve-year-old I'd last seen a decade ago.

She was downright stunning. No one could resist her that night, each of the single men attempting to woo her at some point.

And having her bleeding inches from me?

My hands lengthened into claws, a new wave of desire buffeting me.

If not for her phone, I would have taken her, would have thrown away over forty years of friendship just to taste her lips and feel the beating pulse under her skin. My throat dried out, the telltale ache of hunger cutting like sandpaper as I tried to swallow. Yeah, she would have just loved that. Her instant, disgusted negation of what her friends had asked was warning enough. She was the forbidden apple, the fruit designed to taunt and tempt. I'd never been closer to actually sealing my fate than when she'd stood from that barstool.

Never in my life had I been so grateful for a piece of technology.

The small main road through the mountain town came into view at last, and I finally slowed my pace. One sole building had lights on despite the early afternoon hour. It was only then I realized just how intense the snow truly was, how quickly it was accumulating on the roads and trees and roofs. I eased toward the only building with signs of life.

A middle-aged man exited out the front door, turning to engage both locks before pulling his scarf up to cover his nose. With a practiced ease, I closed the distance between us, brushing my hand against the skin of his cheek to give the command to wordlessly follow me into the alley. He went willingly.

I didn't bother with decorum, didn't worry about who might see. I quietly tilted his head, eased his scarf down, and sank my fangs between the delicate tendons of his throat. Exactly where that prick had bitten her. I drank long and deep—until the sandpaper feel was gone—and then closed the wounds and sent the man back to his life entirely oblivious.

The hunger was gone, just like this morning. And yet I still ached for her, still desired the forbidden fruit, no better than Adam in the garden.

* * *

Nearly a foot of snow fell overnight, only easing for about an hour right before sunrise. When the watery gray light of the sun washed across the bright white powder of the new snow, I set about my typical morning routine. I shrugged on one of my sweaters but didn't bother switching from my heavy sleeping pants. My throat ached in that dull way it did most mornings, the near-constant prick of pain that reminded me I was something other than human and had been from the moment I was born. I rolled my shoulders and stretched my neck, trying to center myself.

Even more important than my morning tea was eating something filling, something that would help stave off the thirst until some of the others arrived this morning and we could go find blood hosts as a collective.

The cabin was quiet as I slowly descended the stairs, though that didn't really surprise me. Even if others had arrived yesterday evening after I'd exiled myself to the small bedroom I'd been assigned, I knew it was much too early for most to be awake. I was always the earliest riser among our friends, and I didn't regret it. I valued the peace of the early morning when the world wasn't quite ready to wake.

There was a prescient silence this morning, though, that had the hairs on the back of my neck rising. Almost like the cabin was waiting for something to happen, knew that something was about to transpire and waited with bated breath.

The snow picked up in the time it took me to get to the kitchen, and large, fat flakes fell in a heavy blanket as I quietly set about making my morning tea. My phone vibrated just as I set the leaves to steep and went to start on the oatmeal.

"Hello, Joshua," I murmured. "I thought you were getting in last night."

My friend scoffed loud enough I could practically feel the eye roll that must have accompanied it. "Don't start with me. Meridith has already been chewing me out all morning about waiting too long and getting behind the weather."

I frowned and leaned a hip against the counter. "Did they close the roads?"

"Unfortunately," he groused. "Full whiteout because of the wind. The pass has been closed since about dinner last night."

Bloody hell. No wonder the town was all-but-closed when I went searching for a host last night.

"Do they have an idea when it will reopen?"

It was less than a week until Christmas. It would be a logistical nightmare if it stayed closed for more than a couple days.

"They're saying another day at least, maybe two. This storm has decided to just hunker down."

"Damn."

"Yeah, tell me about it." Joshua laughed, but it wasn't a happy sound. "So we'll be up in a couple days. Try not to have a rager while we're gone."

I rolled my eyes. "We didn't have ragers when we were young enough to think they were a half-decent idea. I'll just take the time to get caught up on my dissertation students. You be safe getting up here."

When he hung up, I quietly ate the oatmeal, not bothering to sit at the island. It soothed the worst of the hunger, the way any normal food did, though it didn't touch the burn in the back of my throat. Somewhere in the last sixty years, it had become normal, just like any other piece of me. Some vampires never adjusted, though, especially those who were Created rather than born.

Once the bowl and spoon were drying, I pulled the tea leaves from my water and headed deeper into the cabin, seeking out the smaller living room. It had the view I liked most, a sliver of the valley framed by the large pines and unobstructed by any of the other nearby cabins.

The tea was hot, and it helped balance the ache in my throat.

Movement had me pausing just a few steps into the cozy room, a flash of red that had my breath catching. Harlowe glanced up from a book, the title obscured by her hold on the cover. Her cheeks flushed in awkward embarrassment. The bandage on her throat was gone, the bites now an angry, shiny pink that looked like they might scar despite Meridith's wound tonic. Anger flashed in my stomach, but I pushed it down.

"Sorry," I offered. "I didn't realize anyone else was up yet."

Harlowe shrugged. "You're fine. I'm often the only one up. Tessa and Rhiannon are both night owls."

I tucked away that bit of information, hoarding it in the small mental folder I pretended didn't exist, that deplorable part of me that desired my best friend's daughter.

"And besides, everyone got stuck on the other side of the pass. Dad convinced everyone to wait and leave together." Her focus returned to the book, and she turned a page. "The snow came in too heavy and windy for the crews to keep up with it all. Even the town is shut down right now."

Panic flashed across my skin, a wildfire raging across dry scrubland.

No one else was here? And the town wasn't open, either?

My throat burned all over again, stronger than even yesterday afternoon. As if my body knew she was the closest vein, the only reasonable possibility for the foreseeable future, it ratcheted my thirst higher at a rate I hadn't felt in years—*decades*.

All at once, the cabin transformed from a place of tranquility to a snowed-in, forced proximity nightmare, a test of willpower I couldn't hope to survive. Like Eve with that apple, I would break down at some point. I would listen to the wretched voice inside me that begged to taste her—to know just exactly how her dhampir blood would taste against my tongue—consequences be damned. It had been hounding me for months, and the first test of fixing those damn bites was nearly a fail in its own right.

"Ah, I see," I said, my voice hoarse.

She frowned, her eyebrows lowering in confusion, but I didn't trust myself anywhere near her. Not when my throat already held the steady ache of thirst.

I backed out of the room. With shaking hands, I left the mug of tea on the kitchen island. I didn't bother to grab my coat before fleeing into the heavy snow. Again.

Chapter Five

Harlowe

The morning inched by in minutes that seemed to stretch longer with each accumulated hour. The book I'd brought served as a decent distraction for the first hour or so until Landon stepped into the living room. All at once, those butterflies filled my stomach and made it near-impossible to remember how to breathe. His blatant panic at being stuck here with me for the next day or two was a real hit to the self-esteem.

"Yes, just what every woman wants: an attractive man that can't stand the idea of being anywhere near her," I muttered. "The cherry on top is that he's been your crush since you could realize what exactly those were. Just freaking *perfect.*"

I turned the page, trying to settle back into the viking history book. Tessa had gotten it for my birthday the previous month, and it was shaping up to be one of my favorites on the subject. Unfortunately, it was impossible to focus on the words anymore. All I could manage to see when I stared at the pages was the look of utter horror on Landon's face.

With a sigh, I finally admitted defeat and dropped the book onto the end table.

The healing wounds on my neck itched something fierce. I clasped my hands behind my back to keep from messing with the newly formed scabs. I had no interest in bleeding anymore on this holiday trip if I could help it. My phone lit up with a notification where it sat, a silent sentinel beside my abandoned book.

A whole new wave of nerves hit my chest and stole my breath. Racing up the stairs, I called Tessa, knowing she was better at answering than Rhiannon.

She answered on the second ring. Her hair was pulled back, and she was in an oversized sweater.

"Did you get it?" she asked without preamble.

"I haven't opened it."

She sucked in a breath, and then she was moving, too, the background blurring with her vampiric speed. There was noise on the call, and then Rhiannon's voice cut through.

"Did she get it?"

Tessa nodded and urged her over. She was dressed similarly to Tessa, an oversized sweater and flared leggings. Her hair is pulled back again, a messy pile on the top of her head.

"Oh my gosh!" Rhiannon said. "What did it say?"

"She hasn't opened it," Tessa explained.

I closed the door to the large bedroom even knowing I was the only one here. With careless hands, I propped my phone against the nightstand's lamp and then dug through my bag until I could grab my laptop. My hands shook, and my breathing was way too shallow. God, I was going to throw up.

Maybe this internship really was what I was missing. It certainly seemed like it based on my sudden, overwhelming anxiety over the result sitting in my email at the moment.

"Breathe, Harlowe," Tessa said, quiet but firm. "Whatever it says, it's what the universe wants of you right now. You are strong and capable. You are destined for whichever choice the panel made."

"Yes, exactly," Rhiannon added. "The moon guides everyone, knowing or unknowing. This will be good news."

I took a steadying breath and closed my eyes, focusing my own affirmations. I double checked that my best friends could see my screen, and then I opened the email.

It took a long, silent minute for me to absorb what it said. Rhiannon squealed first, and then I shrieked. My laptop fell out of my lap as I leaped to my feet and grabbed my phone. Both of them were laughing and hugging each other.

"You're going to France!" Rhiannon said excitedly, a grin brightening her face. Tessa's mirrored hers.

"I'm going to France," I echoed. My own smile felt like it might split my face, all of the nerves falling away from me in a sudden rush. Not even Landon's freak out was enough to dampen the moment. "I'm going to freaking *France*."

* * *

I coasted through the morning, the happy warmth of excitement about getting the internship bolstering me even as the snow continued to come in large, sweeping sheets. It was almost enough to ignore the small part of me that noticed Landon hadn't returned from wherever he had gone. Tessa, Rhiannon, and I chatted for over an hour, coming up with the best ways to tell my parents. With their promise that they would grab the supplies for the present we came up with, I settled in for a simple lunch in prep for starting all of the paperwork.

And, God, was there a lot of paperwork. By the middle of the afternoon, I was buried in the bureaucracy of it all. Travel plans and visas. Housing and banking. There was a required French language course I hadn't completed during undergrad that took me nearly a half hour to just sort out when and where it would be possible to complete while there. And then there was all the information and permissions I needed to gather as a dhampir. Agreement from the nearest vampire clan. Acknowledgement from the local coven. Signing all of the secrecy laws and local ethic codes.

By the time the front door opened, my eyes vaguely ached and a headache pulsed just behind my temples. My stomach churned with hunger. The bites itched and almost burned, the anti-itch cream I'd put on after the call with the girls having faded. I looked up from my laptop, shocked to find the sun setting, the snow seemingly endless.

Landon stopped just inside the kitchen, his entire body frozen as our gazes locked. His cheeks were flushed a dark red from the cold, and snow slowly melted off his shoulders and head.

"Get your steps in?" I asked, keeping my voice dry, trying to break the oppressive silence.

He snorted, rolled his eyes, and then crossed to the fridge. He pulled together ingredients and turned on the stove, not saying a word as he made a small batch of spaghetti. I couldn't help but stare at him, the rest of the paperwork in front of me forgotten. He wore a different sweater than yesterday, this one a deep forest green that was nearly identical to his eyes. Instead of slacks, he wore thick sweats, the kind skaters used to keep warm when not directly on the ice rink.

He looked so damn good. It should be illegal for anyone to be that attractive after doing only God knew what in the blizzard all damn day. That slow, rolling heat flared out from my belly, and I clenched my thighs on instinct.

Without thinking, I scratched the bite marks. One of the scabs ripped open.

"Ah shit," I muttered.

Landon turned around in an instant, his eyes catching on my hand in a matter of seconds. He scowled, abandoning the half-finished food, and pulled the wound care bin from the cabinet, bringing the entire thing over to me. I didn't wait for him to help me, though, quickly pulling a pack of gauze and pressing it to the bites, hoping he'd stay that full step and a half away from me for the sake of my sanity. My throat was dry already, and my stomach swirled with new nerves.

Luckily, it only took a few minutes of applying pressure for the bleeding to stop and my skin to scab over again. I carefully poured out two drops of Mom's healing tonic, wanting something a bit more secure than just a scab. God knew I would manage to forget again and scratch it during the night.

The entire time, Landon didn't utter a word.

I tried to say something again, tried to keep him from realizing how my body was responding to him just being in the room. "Hovering over me is just as bad as snarling, by the way."

He still didn't say anything. Finally, I risked looking at him. He stood across from me, his hands clutching the island, his knuckles white. His eyes were locked on the bites, his eyes slowly flicking between the bright red and jewel green. Even as his jaw clenched, there was a small flash of his fang against his lower lip.

Understanding hit me like a freight train.

Of course vampires needed blood daily if their hosts were purely human. Had he not found a single host while gone today?

"You're thirsty." It was a statement, but my voice was breathy enough it came across a bit unsure.

He sucked in a breath, his eyes staying red for an entire minute before flicking back and forth again. His nails lengthened, the telltale claws sharpening and pressing into the stone surface of the counter. And still, his eyes didn't drift from where the bites on my neck no longer bled.

"Landon?" I asked, trying to keep from making him feel defensive.

I was used to vampires and their hungers, yes, but I'd also seen what that unchecked power could do—not including dumbass cafe dude. Tessa hadn't lost control often, but the moments I'd seen were enough to leave a permanent etching on my mind. My brother's moments were even worse.

His chest rose, and then his eyes did, too, locking with mine. "Yes."

"You need to feed." Again, a statement a bit too breathy to come across as confident. My thighs clenched at the idea of his lips pressing against my throat, of his fangs sinking into my skin. I'd never let a vampire with a beard feed from me. Would it scratch me?

"Yes." It was a guttural, primal groan.

Lightning shot straight down my spine and tightened my nipples, but I tried to breathe through it. He wouldn't want anything more than my blood, but I couldn't seem to care at the moment. I knew I only ever offered my vein if I would get pleasured, if it would lead to something carnal. But I didn't dare entertain that thought now. Just knowing the feel of his bite would be enough to fantasize about for years, a memory I would hold close in the quiet, dark moments.

Without a word, I held out my wrist in invitation.

His fangs grew even longer, cutting into his bottom lip.

"Joshua will kill me."

I rolled my eyes with a huff. "Dad doesn't need to know what I choose to do with my own body. I'm an adult. I'm able to consent."

I twisted my wrist in renewed offer.

He edged around the island, his movements the barely leashed power I'd seen the night before. They were a more polished version of the vampire at the cafe. His body was a wall of heat, only a foot away from me now. My core pulsed with a renewed, aching interest. Somehow, I managed to keep my hand from trembling.

His hands were gentle as he cradled my wrist and lowered his head over the delicate skin just under my palm. He paused, his lips hovering a bare inch above my skin, for a suspended, infinite moment of time. And then he struck, the same lethal speed I'd felt Tessa use when we were in high school and I had confessed to her I wanted to know what it felt like to be a blood host.

I gasped, the pain cutting through the heat drumming inside my body.

Chapter Six

Landon

Strawberries.

The taste hit me before I could even remove my fangs from the delicate skin of her offered wrist. Her blood tasted like fucking *strawberries*. Ah hell, that was why the kitchen had smelled like a damn strawberry shortcake yesterday. How could I have forgotten that it wouldn't taste like a typical human? She was a dhampir, a half vampire. Her blood would have a unique smell and taste, just like any other vampire.

Even if I had remembered, of all the possibilities, I never would have predicted strawberries. Not when everything about her was so damn fierce, so determined and capable. Not when she was the forbidden fruit, the apple dangled in front of me until I broke.

And, God, did I break.

A mournful groan fell from my lips as I took a step closer

and adjusted my hold on her wrist, bringing it more fully against my mouth. The second swallow was even more decadent than the first, and it silenced that voice shrieking in the back of my mind warning that all of this would end poorly. That swallow only fueled a desire to drink again, and so I did, taking steady, greedy gulps as I crowded those last few inches between us. My knee wedged between hers, and she sucked in a breath.

And then she whimpered.

Horror seized me, freezing my tongue and my throat.

Bloody hell, my fangs were still in her wrist. When was the last time I'd been so enamored with the taste of someone's blood I'd forgotten to pull my fangs away from the punctures? Not since I was a young boy still feeding at my mother's wrist.

I pulled away at once, ready to admit this was the exact poor decision I knew it would be. The blizzard wouldn't last forever. I could hold out. Even as I thought the words, my fangs elongated and a deeper hunger ripped through my body. I couldn't bring myself to move more than a few inches away from the vein I'd opened in her arm.

Harlowe's cheeks were flushed a deep crimson, the same color that spread across her neck and collarbones. Her eyebrows lowered as she bit her lip.

"Is..." Her throat rippled with a swallow. "That can't have been enough. It's never been that fast before."

Jealousy ripped through me, so intense it was a miracle my skin didn't flay right open. How often had she offered her vein that she would know what most vampires needed from a host? From *her*? Between one heartbeat and the next, the need to find that nameless prick and drive a stake through his still-beating heart overwhelmed me. Every muscle tensed in readiness.

Good God above, this was madness.

"Landon?"

Shit, she needed to stop saying my name. I couldn't fucking think straight with the way her lips wrapped around the syllables pinging around in my mind. Uncertainty flashed in her eyes and pinched the corners of her mouth before she reached out to me with her free hand. I didn't trust myself to move, to do anything but hover above her bleeding wrist. She carefully palmed the nape of my neck, her touch light as a feather.

Her chest shuddered with another heavy breath. Thirst and need ripped through me all over again, stronger and deeper than even a moment before.

"It wasn't enough," she whispered.

Her voice had gone low and sultry, her body already reacting to the pleasure my bite always induced. It sent a thrill straight to my cock.

This was such dangerous territory. Another minute, another taste, and I knew I wouldn't trust myself to make the proper choice: leave her untouched in every way that Joshua would use to justify putting a stake through my chest.

That one taste would have to be enough to get me through the next twenty-four hours until the snow slowed enough that the mountain town reopened. I would need those swift, greedy tastes to last long enough to find a human who wouldn't remember me the moment my fangs left their vein, just like the man last night.

As if she could read my thoughts, Harlowe's nails pricked my skin. Her body straightened, as if she had decided something in the stretch of silence. I readied to drop her wrist, to allow her to back off. Instead, she pressed the bleeding punctures to my mouth. The wounds were still bleeding freely, dual beads slowly dripping toward her elbow. I cautiously licked one trail, cleaning the bright red from her skin.

Her breath caught, and both of her hands fisted, the one on my neck twisting into my hair, holding me immobile. Her command wrapped around me, the single word reaching into the depths of me and ripping out the very last bit of common sense by the roots.

"Feed."

I was lost. I settled my lips over the punctures and drank. Each intoxicating swallow was the sweetest nectar, a balm that soothed the biting pain of the thirst more effectively than any human blood could. In a matter of seconds, the sandpaper burn in my throat was gone entirely. And yet I continued to drink, needing to take her deeper, needing to taste her until she was embedded in my bones.

God, it had been decades since I had allowed myself to drink from another preternatural. The memory paled in comparison to Harlowe's sweet, delectable blood.

And with every pull and suckle of my mouth, her body strung tighter. The aphrodisiac nature of my bite overrode her distaste of me, needling deeper the longer I kept her vein open and pulled her blood into my body. A sick, horrid part of me slowed my swallows, forcing the feeding longer so I could keep her next to me, keep her skin against my lips, keep the pleasure growing in her body.

Her breathing grew choppy as she let her head fall back, her eyes fluttering closed. Her fisted hand relaxed into my hair, twisting strands around her fingers. It was a proprietary grip, holding me against her skin. I couldn't hold back the hum of satisfaction at proof my bite was pleasuring her. Even if it was only biology, even if it would fade in the hour after this forced feeding ended. In this moment, I could pretend it was her arousal in truth, that every subtle adjustment of her legs and and scratch of her nails was fueled by her wanting me and not the base response to a vampire's bite.

Just like her blood, I drowned in the fantasy.

It wasn't until her grip on my hair slackened that I pulled away with a rueful sigh. I swiped my tongue over both punctures, making damn sure they were fully sealed. No way was I going to leave her with a mess like that dumbass prick. Her hand slipped out of my hair as I straightened, coasting down my arm.

Her eyes were half-lidded, hazy with desire. Her lips parted, and her cheeks flushed even darker than before. I couldn't look away as I licked the last drop of her blood from my lip, not ready to lose the strawberry taste. Her nails dug into my forearm, and then her wrist twisted out of my hold.

I had one heartbeat to hate myself, to reel in disgust at my assumption she would let my bite sway her toward wanting me. One heartbeat, and then she had my palm against her lips, her eyes still locked on mine. A small flick of her tongue, and I groaned. I let myself trace her lip with my thumb and palm her cheek.

A small smile tilted her lips, and her eyes closed entirely.

No, I couldn't let this happen.

It was just her natural reaction to me feeding from her. The last thing I wanted was to have her wake up tomorrow ashamed that she succumbed to all of this.

I gently freed my hand from her grip. Her lips drew into a pout, but she didn't look at me.

"Landon?" Even her voice was lower, breathier. "Landon, please."

Bloody hell, I shouldn't. Taking her blood was one thing. I could explain that to her father, could make him understand the need. He would, too. As irritated as he would inevitably be that his daughter was the host, he would understand the impossibility of waiting. Every vampire had a story about needing to feed in the worst situation.

But this? Touching Harlowe, sating the need my drinking has stoked in her body? In no possible scenario would he forgive me this. Harlowe's nails bit into my forearm as she tried to drag me back to her. Her eyes fluttered open. The bright, heavy look stole my breath.

There was no worry, no hesitation. There was only a woman who craved, who squirmed in her seat because she needed an orgasm, desired it with every cell in her body.

"Kiss me," she ordered on a whisper.

"Ah Christ."

I cradled her face in my hands, stroking my thumbs across her cheek bones, counting each freckle dotted across them. She twisted a hand under my sweater, her palm spreading across my stomach.

My words were nothing more than a growl fueled by a year's worth of unholy craving.

"Fuck it."

And then I slammed my lips to hers.

Chapter Seven

Harlowe

Landon Rhodes was kissing me.

The thought still felt impossible, but his lips were soft and full against my own. They carried that faint taste of mint and strawberries, like a summer cocktail. It was his hands cupping my face, his knees wedging my legs apart as he crowded fully into me, his fangs that scraped against my lips as his tongue delved into my mouth and explored without hesitation.

My body burned with need, long, pulsing waves that built on each other until no coherent thought existed beneath them. I was drowning in desire. It was so consuming, it became all I had ever known, all I would ever know. Despite all the feedings I'd been a part of, all the vampires I'd given my vein to over the last six years, the depth of the bite's induced arousal was shocking.

It had never once felt like this.

Landon ran his tongue along my lip as he pulled away. I couldn't stop the whine that crept up my throat. I wasn't done, couldn't be done. I needed more of him. I needed him to touch me and slake this awful need he'd awoken that I wasn't sure I'd ever recover from.

Bloody hell, she's too damn sweet.

His voice floated into me, his every thought spilling into my mind as I kept my hands pressed against him. For the first time, they didn't feel overwhelming. They added to the waves, pushed the depths of need even deeper until they felt bottomless. My nails dug into his stomach as my entire body clenched, the pulsing heat in my core becoming unignorable. He groaned against me, and a shiver shot down my spine at the masculine sound. His palm slid down until it cupped my neck, his thumb pressing into the sensitive spot just under my ear.

She's panting. For me. Fuck, I need to taste her cunt, too. Need to feel her under me before this wears off and she hates me again.

Oh god. Hate him?

"I don't hate you," I whispered.

It was stupid, responding to his unspoken thought, but I couldn't let him think that, couldn't let him believe I was only like this because of his fangs in my wrist.

I twisted my hand into his sweater and pulled him closer, driven entirely by instinct. This time, his lips weren't softly exploring. They were hot and unyielding as he tasted me again and then started tracing a path across my jaw and down my neck. His tongue brushed over the other punctures, and I groaned. His lips parted over my collarbone, and then he bit the skin there, pulling it between his lips hard enough I knew it would bruise. I gasped at the sudden bite of pain, both of my hands twisting tighter into his sweater. His thoughts cut off all at once.

He moved to my other collarbone and repeated the bite before following the low v of the sweater I wore. He pushed it to the side with his teeth, pulling until my breast was fully bared, my nipple hard and aching through the thin fabric of my bra. And then his hands left my neck, trailing down my sternum. I squirmed in the chair, trying to find a way to put pressure on my clit and release some of the pressure.

"Landon," I gasped. "Oh, God."

He groaned. And then he pushed aside the cup of my bra and closed his lips around my nipple. Every pull on it, every circle of his tongue around the sensitive flesh, echoed in my clit. He let my breast fall from his mouth, and I shuddered as the wetness he left behind made my skin pebble. I cursed as he did the same to my other breast, his lips and teeth and tongue swirling me into a vortex of need I couldn't breathe through. I rolled my hips forward, and he grabbed my knee, forcing me still.

Something inside me broke. I used my hands still twisted in his sweater to push him down, to try and get him to where I needed him so acutely I was convinced I would die from it. He chuckled even as he dropped to his knees. His hands didn't shake at all as he pushed the skirt of the sweater dress up to my hips and then palmed my thighs, forcing them so far apart I felt laid bare.

Without saying a word, I reached down and pulled my panties to the side, not wanting to wait for him to decide what to do with them. His red eyes flashed brighter, and the sharp curve of his claws pricked my skin as they lengthened again.

And then he leaned forward, and his lips and tongue were on me.

His beard scratched at my skin, every small pinprick of almost pain heightening the feel of his tongue tracing the lines of my pussy. Holy God, there was too much sensation already.

I let my free hand dig into his hair, the small brushes of my palm against his scalp giving me partial thoughts that I had no hope of understanding, of focusing on long enough to decipher their meaning. He was relentless, his movements so skilled it should be illegal. His tongue pressed into me, and I moaned.

Whatever part of my brain that could worry that he'd find me too young, too awkward, too brazen was silenced by a growing primal chant I'd never heard before.

More. More. More.

I couldn't tell if they were his thoughts or my own.

"Landon," I gasped. "Oh, God, I'm right there."

Already? That's not enough for me.

Oh, Jesus.

He didn't slow his movements, though. He pressed into me with a single finger and then a second, curling them with a precision that would haunt my every fantasy from here on out. My entire body trembled.

"Come for me, Harlowe. Let me feel it, taste it. Just this once. Let me have it just this once."

His lips closed over my clit, and he sucked. I detonated.

I cried out, my hand fisting in his hair as my vision blurred out. Lightning shot down my limbs as pleasure rocketed through my core. He didn't slow his movements, his fingers fucking me through every wave of pleasure as it buffeted me like I was a rock along the shore, unable to move.

Eventually, minutes or years later, the sensations faded, and my vision and mind returned. I panted, trying to catch my breath. Landon carefully pulled away from me, pulling my hand away from my panties, adjusting them until I was covered again. He eased back onto his heels, his own chest heaving with his breathing. I let go of his hair, scared I'd hurt him.

And then the undeniable need to taste him, feel him in my mouth, to return the pleasure he'd given me, filled me. I scrabbled at his sweater, trying to get myself off the stool and on the floor with him, but he deftly grabbed my hands and forced me still. His eyes were still red, his fangs so long I could see them even as he clenched his jaw. His erection was obvious in his sweats, the line of it impressive. My mouth watered at just the thought of having all of him in my mouth, tasting his skin and feeling him shudder around me.

"Landon," I said, trying again.

He shook his head. "I'm fine, Harlowe."

I swallowed my sudden nerves. I wasn't anywhere near close to a virgin, but his refusal had me questioning everything I'd ever experienced with a man. No one had ever turned down a blowjob. The urge to touch his skin, to sneak away his thoughts, was consuming.

Before I could break out of his hold, though, he took a long breath, and his eyes dropped back to emerald. With soft, careful movements, he twisted my wrist until the punctures were facing up. The skin around them was lightly bruised, a blue-gray that would probably deepen into purple overnight.

It was worse than some bites I'd had, but the wounds were closed. In fact, they were more thoroughly scabbed than the ones the jerk from the cafe had left in my throat yesterday morning. Landon nodded, tracing each puncture with his thumb. I couldn't help but shiver, my pussy clenching all over again, heedless of the orgasm he'd wrung from my body.

His breath caught, and his throat rippled with a swallow. For a brief moment, I thought he'd actually let me put my mouth on him. Instead, he set my arm on my thigh and pulled away.

"Let me go get the cream," he whispered, "before the itching sets in."

He stood in a single, fluid movement that had heat spiking in my veins again. My nipples hardened again, and my cheeks flushed. His eyes caught on them, and the outline of his cock twitched. God, it was only a couple inches from me now.

"You really don't want me to—"

"It's fine," he said, waving me off. "Let me get your wounds cleaned up, and then I'll feed you."

Chapter Eight

Harlowe

My muscles were loose when I woke the next morning, languid and satisfied in a way I hadn't felt since my last situationship in college in the spring.

I layered an oversized sweater over the slip I'd worn to bed, the cabin surprisingly warm given the raging snowstorm still blustering outside, and walked down the hall to the main bathroom upstairs. All of the windows reflected nothing but large swathes of white. The snow hadn't slowed at all, still coming down in heavy sheets, the wind swirling the flakes into a wall of white.

I peeled off the bandages from both bites, dropping the gauze into the trash beside the sink and then washing my hands. Neither set of punctures had opened overnight, so I didn't bother to mess with either of them yet. They could wait until after I'd gotten some caffeine and carbs into my system.

Just as I was starting to comb through my hair, my phone pinged multiple times and then vibrated with a call. One of the girls must have woken up and seen the string of texts I'd sent last night after Landon had finished the forgotten spaghetti and made sure both sets of punctures were bandaged. I supposed the caffeine and carbs would have to wait.

Tessa's face filled the screen when I answered the incoming video call.

"Are you serious?" she asked without preamble.

I twisted my wrist, showing the new set of bites. The bruise had indeed darkened to purple, but the punctures themselves were small and already well on their way to healing. Even the ones in my neck looked better, whatever he'd done when he'd kissed them last night working wonders. Not even Mom's healing tonic could move that fast.

"Holy shit," Tessa breathed, her eyes wide.

"Oh, is it Harlowe?" Rhiannon's voice preceded her face. And then her eyes were wide, too, shock stilling her normally restless body. "*Harlowe.*"

"Don't say anything!" I begged just as Tessa covered her mouth. Rhiannon easily pulled it away, a shit-eating grin curling her lips.

"Was it good?" Rhiannon asked. "Please tell me it was good. That man looks like he knows how to *fuck.*"

"*Rhiannon!*" I grabbed my phone and turned down the volume, looking over my shoulder. "We didn't have sex."

Tessa raised an eyebrow. "Really? But you don't ever

host unless you get an orgasm out of it. The itchiness isn't worth it."

My cheeks flushed like I was a damn virgin, but I rolled my eyes and focused on finishing my hair. "Orgasms are not the same thing as sex, thank you very much."

"Semantics," Rhiannon said, some of her normal excitement creeping back in. She tapped her fingers to an unheard beat. "Was it *good?*"

My chest flushed, too, as I nodded. "Oh, yeah, it was definitely amazing."

Both of them squealed. I couldn't help but grin.

"You have to tell us everything when we get up there!" Rhiannon ordered.

Before I could say anything else, Tessa turned the conversation to the blizzard, her tone conveying everything I needed to know. Someone else was in the room who definitely didn't need to know I'd finally gotten to feel Landon's fangs and tongue last night. I twisted my hair into a messy bun as she spoke, adjusting a few of the pieces until they framed my face, trying to make it seem like this was one of our typical calls. Then I put on my normal makeup: mascara, eyeliner, and lip gloss.

"It's looking like we'll get to head up early tomorrow morning," Tessa said. "Snow should be settling overnight finally. Mom's bringing enough popcorn for garland to drown in, just a warning."

There was a guy's laugh in the background. Rhiannon's eyes narrowed, but she didn't say anything as a third person came onto the screen.

"Hey, H. How are you handling being locked in that cabin?"

Miles Brown, one of my brother's friends, was one of those dumbass vampires that had gotten in a ton of trouble shortly after Landon had moved and joined our local vampire clan last year. His eyes were a brown so dark they often looked black, and his brown hair was cut a little too long to look anything more than disheveled most of the time. He'd been Changed just over five years ago when he was a freshman in college. He gave me the fucking creeps.

I gave a bland smile.

"Fine so far. It's nice and quiet without you up here."

He grinned like the dig was meant to be a joke.

It wasn't.

Tessa pushed him out of the frame.

"Get lost, Brown. This is girl talk time."

Miles threw an arm around Tessa's shoulders, grinning.

"Wish I could, T, but I was sent to grab you. We're all going to get a host so we don't have to go out tomorrow until we're over the pass."

Tessa scrunched her nose and then shoved him away from her. "All right, all right. I'll be done in another couple minutes. Now get *out*."

Rhiannon glared where he had disappeared, her hand clenching and unclenching like she wanted to punch him. Didn't we all?

A door closed downstairs, and my body lit with an electric anticipation. I cleared my throat.

"Perfect. I'll text you guys later, all right?"

Both girls raised an eyebrow, a knowing glint in their eyes, but they didn't dare say anything with Miles still within earshot.

"All right. We'll chat later." Tessa hung up.

Once the screen cleared, I set about taking care of the bites. While the original set in my neck looked leagues better, there was still that underlying itch. It would probably be like that for another few days. Right now, it looked like I might luck out and not have any scarring, so I really didn't want to risk ripping open the new skin. I grabbed the anti-itch cream stashed in the bathroom, under the sink tucked behind the extra hand towels.

The clear cream sank into my skin, alleviating the itch almost instantly, like it was its own version of novocaine for my skin. I washed my hands and then put the cream away, ready to see if Landon needed a host again today. My thighs clenched in anticipation.

Landon. Right.

I twisted my wrist to look at his bite.

His bite didn't itch. It didn't burn. It didn't ignite that desire to try and claw the entire thing out of my skin. He'd put the initial aftercare cream on it the night before, but I hadn't done anything to it this morning. And it still didn't itch.

The realization came slowly, like the slow-rising sun in the east every morning, the changes to the sky subtle and then, all at once, it crests the horizon and lights the world anew.

His bite didn't itch. Which meant...

I swallowed and looked at myself in the mirror, trying to remember how to breathe. There was too much excitement surging through my chest, crashing underneath my sternum. My hands shook with it.

I was Landon Rhodes's Fated. His blood mate.

Chapter Nine

Landon

"I made extra eggs if you'd like some," I said, not turning away from my own plate where it perched beside the sink.

The footsteps on the stairs hesitated for a moment. And then she continued into the kitchen, wordlessly grabbing a plate and scooping the eggs I'd very intentionally made for her onto it.

"Thank you," she said, her cheeks flushing a dark pink as she glanced at me under her lashes.

She quickly ducked her head and walked to the kitchen, sliding into the same barstool she'd perched in the night before. Blood went straight to my dick, the incorrigible thing. I crossed my ankles and tried to ignore it.

Her hair was pulled up today, only a few strands falling along her face and neck. It made the bastard's bite stick out against her pale skin. My fangs extended as the sun reflected off the shiny pink skin.

Bloody hell, this was ridiculous. And I knew it would be like this. The moment I touched her, kissed her, I knew it would dig into me, become something I would always crave. It was why I hadn't let her follow through on the offered orgasm. Just the strawberry taste of her blood was enough to have me spiraling. If she'd added the feel of her hands gripping me? Her tongue tracing me?

My dick twitched in anticipation. I crossed my ankles the other way and twisted a bit more toward the counter.

Harlowe pulled open her laptop and started writing in the notebook she'd been using last night, her breakfast only half-finished.

"I thought you weren't taking classes." I tried to keep my voice neutral, one acquaintance speaking with another. It came out a bit too hoarse for my liking.

She shook her head. "I just found out I got an archeology internship in France. I'm trying to sort through all the logistics."

France.

The word settled in my stomach like a stone, the exact reminder my body needed right now.

"Congratulations. I'm sure Joshua and Meredith are ecstatic."

I shouldn't bring them up, but it was self-preservation at this point. I couldn't keep standing here, watching as her lips folded over the fork tines and her throat moved with every half-forgotten swallow. It was fucking torture.

"They don't actually know yet," she admitted after a

minute, another blush staining her cheeks. "I'm planning on telling them when they get here."

I had no good response to that, most of my blood now in a head that doesn't give a damn about niceties or propriety or any of the other things I'm supposed to care about. I focused on finishing my eggs and then pulling the tea leaves from my mug. Once the breakfast dishes were cleaned and put away, I closed the distance between us.

"Let me see your wrist," I ordered, holding out my hand. The command was too aggressive, the words too hungry, but I was doing my best. Keeping my hard-on away from her watchful gaze was taking most of my self-control right now.

She pursed her lips, her eyebrows drawing low, even as she held up her left wrist without hesitation.

"Do you need more? Sorry, I should have asked you before focusing on all of this."

I shook my head. No, I didn't actually need more of her blood. I wouldn't for days yet, the benefit of her being a preternatural. But if she was offering? My fangs extended at once, my gaze sharpening.

Her breath caught, and the flush rushed down her neck and into her chest. She shifted in her seat, and the collar of her dress moved, revealing a dark bruise straddling her left collarbone.

My mouth went dry.

"Your other wrist," I choked out. "I want to check how the punctures are healing."

She stared at me for nearly a minute, like she didn't understand what I'd asked of her. Indecision flashed in her eyes as she looked down at her wrist and then back up at me.

"It's fine," she said, all of her usual sass missing from her voice. She sounded... scared. "I took care of it upstairs."

She gestured to the punctures in her throat, the clear sheen of the anti-itch cream distorting the newly-closed skin. They looked leagues better than they had last night, my tongue helping heal them, too, despite them being almost two days old.

"Even still," I said, taking a half-step closer. "Let me check on it."

My knee brushed hers. Her chest shuddered, and her pulse beat like a hummingbird in her throat. Fuck, I wanted to taste her strawberry again, feel the warm heat of it on my tongue and down my throat. And then I wanted to taste *her*, chase the strawberry of her blood with the clean, rich taste of her cunt.

My dick was achingly hard again, awoken from the half-asleep place I'd managed to coax it over the last five minutes. Bloody hell.

Her eyes fluttered closed as she offered the wrist I'd fed from. The punctures were clean and scabbed over entirely, the skin around them bruised a deep purple. I'd bitten a bit too deep, not quite piercing her where the damage would be lessened. I couldn't help but stroke my thumb across it. Her palm brushed my forearm with the movement.

She shuddered, her legs squirming like she was uncomfortable. Of course she would be. My bite must be itching to high heaven, and me touching it would only make it worse. I pulled my thumb away but didn't drop her wrist.

"Shit, sorry, I shouldn't have touched it. Let me grab the aftercare cream."

She shook her head. "It's fine. I don't need it."

Don't need it? Why wouldn't she need the anti-itch cream? She'd clearly only applied it to the bite on her neck. Her wrist must be uncomfortable as all hell.

And then it slammed into me, more forceful than a summer gale. God, no wonder I'd been borderline obsessed with her the last year despite all the reasons I knew it was folly in the extreme.

The entire world stopped spinning, I swear to God. There was no snow storm outside, no mug of hot tea perched on the counter across the kitchen, no laptop fan quietly whirring beside her elbow. My brain was the only thing moving, processing at way too fast a speed. Her closed eyes, her resistance to showing me the bite, her shuddering breath and nervous restlessness.

She was my Fated, and she didn't want it.

I dropped her wrist at once and took two steps away from her, shoving my hands into the pockets of my slacks.

"It doesn't need to mean anything." The words were ash on my tongue, but I forced them out anyway, keeping my voice neutral.

There was no reason to leash her to me, to force her into this when she had only offered her vein out of an altruism I could never understand. She was going to France, a brand new career opportunity ahead of her. An entirely new coven and clan, a social network that didn't include surly friends of her father. She would be free to find a mate of her choosing there, someone she didn't hate.

Harlowe stared at me like she was trying to see straight through me, like she wanted to strip away every wall and metaphorical piece of armor until I stood before her truly bare. My stomach clenched, but I kept my face impassive.

An oppressive silence stretched between us. Then, she dropped her head and scooped her things off the counter. Without a word, she left the kitchen, heading deeper into the cabin. A moment later, a door closed with awful, quiet precision.

Something too close to regret crowded my throat and threatened to drown me, but I ignored it.

Chapter Ten

Landon

"The pass is reopening around midnight, so we should be up there by mid-morning tomorrow."

Joshua's voice cut through the room from where my phone was perched on the low dresser, the speaker crackling a bit with whatever Joshua was doing while discussing their new travel plans. I studiously sorted through the dissertation proposals I hadn't reviewed before the winter break, reading the words without actually comprehending them. But anything was better than remembering Harlowe's soft skin and breathy moans while her father tried to talk to me.

Fuck, I was hard again. Thinking about Harlowe. While chatting with her father.

I was going to hell.

"Sounds good," I said, clearing my throat to cover the sudden desperate rasp in my voice.

"I'm sure you're desperate for everything to reopen as well," Joshua said, understanding in his tone now. "We will understand if you're out with a host when we get up there. No need to wait for us to arrive."

A host.

Just the thought of taking some random human's vein to my mouth had me wanting to vomit. All I could picture was Harlowe's soft skin and the mouthwatering taste of her strawberry blood. Saliva surged in my mouth, and my fangs extended between one heartbeat and the next, more than happy to slake the need. Even though my body wasn't actually in need of blood and wouldn't be for several more days.

"Of course," I managed to choke out. And then I steered the conversation away from anything to do with this cabin and this holiday.

He hung up a few minutes later, drawn away by his own chosen mate. Meridith and Joshua weren't Fated, but their love and commitment ran deeper than most I'd ever seen. None of our friends were Fated, actually. It was incredibly rare, not something every person was destined to discover. There were musings by the more philosophical of our kind— of vampires—that not everyone even had a Fated to discover, that it was something that appeared randomly just like any other trait. Much like how some animals were born with albinism. There perhaps was a reason for it to appear, but no one had taken the time to discover just exactly what those causes might be.

I had a Fated.

My stomach clenched with the thought, just as it had every time it coursed across my mind today, pacing in this tiny bedroom like a caged animal myself. I knew myself. I knew I didn't have the self control to resist forcing myself on Harlowe if I saw her. Not with my bite in her wrist and the reality that she was my blood mate hanging in the air between us.

I put down the proposal I had been trying to read for the last half hour, finally admitting defeat. There was no way I could focus on the minutia of my profession, no matter that I found great satisfaction from teaching various aspects of the Middle Ages. This spring I was finally getting to build a course revolving specifically around the Norman Invasion and its long-lasting, rippling effects through the rest of the medieval period in England and Europe as a whole.

A soft knock had my head shooting up.

Harlowe stood against the threshold, still in that charcoal gray sweater and flowing, thin dress beneath it. Her hair was messier than this morning, more strands falling around her face. There was a burning intensity in her gaze, in the set of her shoulders, that hadn't been there this morning. My stomach clenched in dual anticipation and foreboding.

"We need to talk," she said without preamble, that hardline sass back in her voice.

I gathered the papers and dropped them unceremoniously onto the dresser beside my phone. Shoving my hands in my pockets, I propped a hip against the ledge, forcing my body relaxed.

"All right," I said.

She hesitated, her teeth biting into the plush skin of her bottom lip. My dick twitched in renewed interest, but I ignored it entirely. She didn't move from the threshold, her arms wrapped protectively around her stomach.

"You want this to mean nothing?" she asked after a long

silence, no inflection at all in her voice. It was a neutral question, as if she was asking if I had noticed the snow finally starting to slow this afternoon before the sun set.

"I think that might be best," I offered, that same ashy taste on my tongue.

Her lips pursed, and then she shook her head. "You're lying."

"Excuse me?"

Indignation ripped through me. Indignation and fear. How could she possibly know that the last thing I wanted was for this to mean nothing, that what I really wanted was to splay her out across this bed and claim her in every way possible between two people. Nevermind that we'd both done all of that countless times before with others. I needed her body pliant under mine, needed her cunt clenching down around my cock and not just my fingers, needed to feed from her as I brought her to an indescribable orgasm.

"I said you're lying." This time, there was fire in the words. She took a step into the bedroom and dropped her arms. "I know that you wanted to do more than just eat me out last night. I know that you want to announce to the clan that I'm your Fated."

All the blood drained from my face. "You know nothing."

She rolled her eyes and then held out her hand, palm up. My bite was still bruising her skin, and it had that ravenous, primal hunger that had nothing to do with my blood thirst roaring up in me.

"Yes, I do." She took another step closer, and I scowled, unable to pry my eyes away from my twin punctures. "It's my gift."

That had me focusing on her face again. It hadn't even occurred to me that she might have a gift that would present like this. How could I have forgotten that all dhampirs had a special gift, the amalgamation of their unique genetics?

"You're a verifier?"

It was a mediocre term for the ability some dhampirs had: the ability to know the truth of what someone said. The ability was more or less strong depending on the person. Some had to touch you to know, a living lie detector in truth. Others could taste a lie but not the truth. Each was wholly different, just like the dhampirs themselves.

She shook her head. Her gaze dropped to her hand as she clenched it and then spread it flat again. "I'm a reader."

Holy fucking bloody hell.

Surprise ripped through me, my mouth dropping open.

Readers were practically myth, something discussed but never actually encountered. I couldn't think of a single dhampir in the last century with a gift that fell under the umbrella term. I always thought it was a lucky thing, too. Being inundated with the thoughts of those around you sounded miserable. There was no privacy even when you wanted to provide it, even when all you wanted was quiet.

Harlowe was quick to continue, her words falling over each other.

"It's by touch only, just in my palms. My palms have to touch bare skin, and then it's only the surface thoughts. I'm not able to, like, dig around or anything. I don't see images or anything, either. I just hear thoughts, just the words themselves."

All at once, small behaviors fell together, morphing into a coherent picture. Her careful reserve with everyone, even her own parents. The quick grimaces when she thought no one was looking and the ones that made her seem uncomfortable with the person she was greeting.

And then her odd comment last night suddenly clicked into place.

"That's why you said you didn't hate me," I said. My voice was oddly detached despite everything spiraling inside me. "You were touching me when I thought that. You…"

Bloody hell. How much else had she heard?

"I'm sorry," she whispered. "It's not something I can stop. If I want to touch someone… if I want to feel their skin against mine…"

Her eyes closed and her throat rippled with a swallow.

"So tell me the truth, Landon," she said, her voice suddenly strong and full of demand. "I deserve to know it."

All at once, the desire I'd tried to hold back all day, the primal need to know my Fated in every possible way, in every possible iteration, swept through me. My fangs elongated, and my claws lengthened. My dick was so fucking hard it ached.

Her eyes brightened, but she didn't back down. "What do you really want, Landon? Do you want this to mean nothing?"

In answer, I crowded her into the doorway, lifted her until I could press my hips against hers, and buried my fangs in the unmarred side of her throat.

Chapter Eleven

Harlowe

The strike was blinding, stealing every single bit of breath from me. I couldn't scream, couldn't cry out, couldn't demand he apologize. For one infinite, horrid second, my entire world was nothing but white hot pain.

And then it disappeared, flowing out into my limbs as a pulsing electricity. It settled in my core, my clit throbbing with it. My body melted against his, need sweeping through me like a flash flood, leaving me unable to resist a single speck of it.

His lips were hot and demanding against my throat, each pull from my vein a new shock of arousal in my bloodstream. I clawed at his back, trying to get him closer, needing to channel all of this desire he ratcheted so tightly in my body in the span of seconds.

His cock was hard and heavy against my belly, his hips

moving against mine giving me a damn good idea of how he wanted to fuck me. I dug my nails into the skin of his neck and used it as leverage, rocking my own hips, too. He groaned against my throat. His hands were hot brands on my thighs, holding me up and open for him. It was so primal, so overtly controlling. I'd never been manhandled quite like this. I shuddered, surrendering to it, to him.

More. More. More. Need to feel her under me. Need to have her lips on me.

His thoughts flowed into me again, and I moved my palm back to his shoulder, to where his sweater covered his skin.

His tongue swiped over the bite, and then he was pulling us both away from the threshold, my lips bracketing his hips in reaction to the sudden movement. He dropped me onto the bed, his eyes bright red, his cheeks hollower than before, his nostrils flared wide with his shuddering breaths.

I sat up and stripped out of the sweater and slip, letting them fall to the side of the bed. His eyes grew brighter as his gaze trailed down my body, taking in every swell and freckle. A low, rumbling growl emanated from him, the sound entirely male satisfaction. My nipples hardened, and I swallowed an answering whimper. He stripped out of his own clothes faster than I could truly track, his movements a blur of limbs and fabric. And then he stood at the foot of the bed, a silver condom packet in his clenched hand, his dick jutting up toward his stomach.

I crawled toward him, ready to touch him, to feel him, to know what he would feel inside me. Fated were supposed to be the epitome of pleasure, and I wanted to know if that was the truth in reality. Surprise lit through me as I settled on my knees in front of him, my hand replacing his at the root of his dick.

"You're pierced?" The question was way too breathy given my very much *non*-virgin status.

His chuckle was dark. It rumbled through the room. His hands were soft where they buried into my hair, undoing the elastic and pins that kept my hair piled on top of my head.

"They won't bite, Harlowe," he said, running his hands through my hair and leaving it to drape over my shoulder, hiding the other vampire's bite entirely. "That's my job, remember?"

I shivered and my pussy clenched around nothing.

Carefully, I traced my fingers over the silver piercings that ran along the underside of his dick. Four separate piercings, all an inch or so apart with another inch or two above the final rod before the head.

"I've never..." I pressed my thumb into the small indent just below the crown, fascinated by all the metal. His dick twitched. "I've never been with someone pierced."

"They won't hurt you," he said, suddenly serious, earnest. "And if for some reason they do, I can take them out."

I let my tongue replace my finger, carefully feeling each one. The metal was surprisingly warm, the skin soft and yet hard around them. With each swipe, each brush, Landon tensed above me, his hand clenching and relaxing and then clenching again at his sides. His nails were fully claws, his control over their appearance shattered. His breathing was stuttered.

Finally, I closed my lips around his head and slowly took him deep, relaxing my tongue. The feelings of the piercings were fascinating, foreign but not uncomfortable. He groaned, his head falling back. When he hit the back of my throat, I swallowed on instinct, suppressing my gag reflex.

"Oh shit, oh shit," he muttered. His hips flexed, his stomach rippling with the movement. "Bloody hell, Harlowe."

I couldn't help but smile even as I kept moving, circling his base with one hand, making sure none of him was missing out. It was a heady thing, watching a vampire's control fall away and collapse around them. But knowing it was Landon Rhodes, the surly man who was known for his iron-clad ethics and control? It was intoxicating, addicting. It ruined me for anyone else again.

He shuddered, and his stomach clenched. He pulled away from me, a hand on my chin keeping me from going after him. Without a word, he handed me the condom. My hands were surprisingly steady as I rolled it on and then laid on the bed, not bothering to move any of the blankets. He followed me, covering me with his body and his heat.

He filled me with a single stroke, so intense I lost my breath. He laid love bites down my sternum, pulling small pieces of skin between his teeth until they were bright red and stinging. I knew they would bruise. His beard scratched against my skin, leaving it raw, too. Every mark he wanted to give, I wanted to take.

Pleasure coursed through me as he moved above me, moved in me, his body a formidable mass of capable muscle. His thumb circled my clit, small, strong circles that had me falling over the ledge before I even realized I was standing on the precipice. My back bowed as I cried out. I desperately clutched at his sides, forgetting entirely my gift.

He didn't, though.

Fuck, you're beautiful like this. So soft. So warm. I need you to come again.

"Come again, Harlowe. I need another one."

I shook my head, letting my hands drop away from him. My body was too overwhelmed, my nerve endings already at their limit. He growled something I couldn't understand, my mind still fuzzy from the sudden orgasm. He pulled away from me, his body disappearing.

I gasped, fear clenching my heart.

And then he was there again, rolling me onto my knees, guiding me until I straddled his hips. He sat against the headboard, our chests pressed together. Every brush of his skin against my over-sensitized nipples had me shivering, my pussy clenching.

"Ride me," he ordered.

He held his dick for me as I settled over him, took him in one full stroke that stole my breath. Holy *God*. I fisted my hands on my thighs, clenching my stomach to keep my balance.

"Touch me," he whispered.

I couldn't resist the quiet command. I spread my hands along his shoulders, my nails digging into his skin with every rough slide of his dick in me. His fangs were so long, cutting into his bottom lip, but he didn't seem to mind. His thoughts flowed through me again, an endless stream of praise and commands that blurred together the more my body tightened toward a second release.

"You're close?" he asked.

When I nodded, he palmed my hips, fucking up into me faster than I'd dared to go. I dropped my head back, the sensations too much. He wrapped a hand in my hair and tilted my head. His fangs sank into my neck, right over the very first bite that hadn't healed right.

Stars exploded behind my eyes. I screamed, my knees collapsing. My weight fell on Landon, but he didn't seem to mind, his hips moving wildly underneath me, his own groan a balm to my very soul.

It took several breathless minutes for me to realize he hadn't actually pulled from my vein the second time. He ran his tongue over the new punctures, a low, satisfied growl rumbling through his chest.

"The only vampire allowed to mark you is me," he whispered against the wounds. "Understand?"

I clenched around him, goose bumps flooding my skin. Slowly, I nodded.

"Only you, Landon."

And, God, it felt like a dream to be able to say that, to be able to promise him my vein.

Chapter Twelve

Harlowe

I awoke in Landon's bed, draped over him like a weighted blanket. His dick dug into my belly, jumping as I slowly rolled off of him. His hands tightened around me for a moment before relaxing again. His face was beautiful like this, smoothed with sleep, the early morning sun playing across his warm skin. I settled back against him, curving into his side and resting my nose against his throat.

My phone vibrated, but I ignored it. All I wanted right now was to bask in the heady, happy feelings of knowing I was in Landon's bed with his bites on my throat. Bites that didn't itch.

"You keep making that noise, and I'll think you're awake enough for more interesting activities." His voice was so low, so hoarse. It sent a shiver all its own down my spine.

I couldn't help but smile into his skin. After another minute, his breathing relaxed back into the cadence of heavy sleep. My phone vibrated again. With a sigh, I crawled over to the nightstand and flipped it over. Tessa's name flashed on the screen with an incoming call. I watched as it went to voicemail, and then a message from Rhiannon came through.

> We're on the pass! Will be there in about an hour.

A new worry clawed in the pit of my stomach, erasing the happy warmth of a moment ago. I eased out of Landon's bed, slipping into the thin dress I'd worn most of yesterday and holding the sweater in my arms. My body ached in the best ways. I turned back to him and pressed a kiss under his ear.

"I'm going to get ready. The pass and roads are open."

He mumbled something I couldn't understand, reaching for me, but I kept out of his hold. No way was I risking anyone showing up while I still looked like I'd been fucked within an inch of my life. After a minute, he rolled onto his side with a heavy sigh.

The cabin was still and silent as I showered and slipped into a new dress, one with a high turtle neck that would hide most of Landon's bites. I left my hair to air dry, running my brush through it only long enough to work through the tangles.

The nervousness was getting worse.

I pulled out the ingredients for molasses crinkle cookies, needing to keep my hands busy. Some people ran to steady their nerves, some drank alcohol. Me? I baked. I settled into the easy rhythm and tried to forget everyone that would be here in just another hour or so.

I'd finished the first dough and set it to rest in the fridge when Landon walked in. He wore the same sweater as that first day with a pair of jeans. His beard was freshly trimmed, the lines stark against his face. He came straight to me, wrapping his arms around my waist and pressing a kiss into the crook of my shoulder. I pulled the bowl off the stand mixer and scraped the sides, giving it all one final mix before dropping it into a clean bowl to rest as well.

"Everyone is almost here," I said. The panic was there, in my voice, making it quiver.

He tensed, ran his nose along the newest punctures he'd made. "I know."

He pulled the bite marks between his teeth, sucking on them. I gasped, heat spooling out from my core like he'd bitten me in truth.

"Landon," I gasped, letting my hands drop to the counter.

"Don't worry, baby. I'll take away the ache."

Baby. Where the hell had that come from? And why did I like it?

I didn't bother trying to figure it out.

With a palm on the small of my back, he eased me over the counter. The skirt of my dress rose high on my thighs, and he growled in approval. His hands trailed up my legs, feather light against my skin. I grabbed the edge of the counter as he guided me onto my tip toes, my hold tight enough to whiten my knuckles. My body practically shook in anticipation.

When was the last time I felt this level of need? This all-consuming desire that left me willing to be taken in a public part of my parents' cabin?

The honest answer was never.

He dropped to his knees, his hands brands on my inner thighs. His lips were hot, his tongue irresistible. It took him only minutes to get me right to the edge, dangling over it.

"Landon," I gasped, digging my hand into his hair. "Oh God, please."

"I know," he said. "I know."

He eased one finger inside me and then a second. He curled them, and my entire being quaked. When he did it a second time, he bit the inside of my thigh, his fangs piercing the skin.

My back bowed as the orgasm ripped through me, stealing my vision and locking my muscles in rapture. I gasped his name, and his lips settled over the bite. Each pull had another aftershock ripping through me until I was a shaking pool of myself, unable to hold my own weight anymore. His tongue swept over the broken skin, and then he stood up. He lay over top of me, pressing a kiss to the base of my neck. I couldn't help the tremors as he slowly undid his belt.

Laughter cut through the cabin, faint but growing stronger. Landon froze. A door closed, and then another, and then my father's voice was joining in on the laughter happening outside.

Landon dropped my dress and stepped away like he'd been burned. Those nerves clawed back up my throat, stronger than ever.

"I'm yours, right?"

I didn't mean to ask it. I'd told him last night to tell me the truth, and he had. He'd told me the truth with his body, with his bite, with him telling me no other vampire was allowed to mark me. I shouldn't need confirmation again this morning. Silence stretched between us. My heart was in my throat.

"Landon?" I looked over my shoulder. His face was frozen in panic and fear. "You said... last night. I'm yours, right?"

He didn't say a word, his red eyes slowly dropping back to green as he looked at me and then toward the front of the cabin. And then he was gone.

The slam of the front door echoed through the entire cabin. Something twisted in my chest, that part of me that held the small, flickering flame of youthful optimism shriveling with the sound. I dropped my cheek to the counter, trying to find the will to stand up, to finish these cookies. Instead, tears slowly cascaded down my cheeks. I traced the small punctures on my inner thigh with a shaking hand, willing them to itch, to burn, to stop being the evidence of a vampire's most coveted connection.

A connection he didn't want.

I swallowed down the wail of emotion building behind my sternum and pushed off the counter.

The flame snuffed out.

※ ※ ※

I'd barely scooped out the first round of dough onto a baking sheet when the front door opened and noise crashed through the cabin. I pressed the back of my hand to my cheeks just to triple check they weren't puffy anymore. I'd taken five minutes in the bathroom to clean up, putting on more makeup than I typically wore to try and hide the red mess left behind by the tears.

Both sets of bite marks on my neck were nearly healed, only a pair of faint pink dots of new skin on either side. The other two bites were hidden by the sweater dress I'd lowered back into place after he left me.

Left me.

The words threatened to tear through the hastily constructed walls around my heart, so I shoved them away. Rhiannon found me first, running straight to me. She took one of the scooped balls of dough and popped it into her mouth.

"Oh my gosh! I could smell the molasses. How can I help?"

I kept my head down, not trusting that my eyes would stay dry. "Probably not by eating one of the cookies," I said, trying to keep my voice dry, trying to say the joke we always said when I was baking and Rhiannon wanted to eat the dough.

Her body froze, all her restless energy dropping into a singularity as she focused on me.

"Harlowe?" she asked, her voice cautious now. "What happened? Why have you been crying?"

She was my best friend. Just because she knew I had been crying didn't mean it was obvious, right? God, I hoped it wasn't obvious. Rhiannon pulled me into her arms, ignoring entirely the metal cookie scoop squished between our bodies. I closed my eyes, the tears burning as I forced them not to fall.

"Here!" Tessa said, her voice bright and happy, too. "Your parents are still outside. I convinced Mom to keep them out there so you had time to set this up. Where do you want…"

She trailed off. Something clinked on the island counter.

And then she was there, too, embracing me while Rhiannon did, running her hands through my hair. She sucked in a startled breath as she saw the new bites.

"Wait, did you two…?"

Voices got louder as more people filed in.

Tessa turned. "Dylan! Keep people outside for a bit longer. We haven't had time to set it up for her parents."

"All right," Dylan said, drawing out the syllables. "You sure you're all okay? Because that doesn't look like happy girl scheming. It looks like sad girl intervention-ing."

"Dylan!" Rhiannon hissed. "Just keep the parental figures outside!"

"Right! Okay! I'll do my best!" His footsteps disappeared back toward the front door. A moment later, it slammed behind him.

Rhiannon pulled me away from her, her eyes bright with anger.

"What did he *do*?"

The words came out stilted, and some tears managed to break free and run down my cheeks. Tessa was quick to wipe them away, her own sadness growing with each part of it all I tell.

"We're F-Fated," I admitted. Both women sucked in a gasp. "The… the bites don't itch. Or burn. Only the first one bruised."

I tilted my head and pulled the turtleneck down to fully show the first one he'd laid the night before, right under my left ear. Tessa stared in shock. Rhiannon slowly traced the bite. I couldn't help but shiver.

"We'll run interference," Tessa said. "You still want to surprise your parents with this? We could wait until tomorrow." She gestured to the bag she'd left on the counter.

I closed my eyes and counted to twenty, trying to reel myself back in.

"Tomorrow. I... Let's do it tomorrow."

Tessa hugged me tight again, pressing her cheek to mine. Another tear fell down my cheek, but Rhiannon wiped it away.

Chapter Thirteen

Landon

Meridith's delighted scream cut straight through me. I leaned against the hallway threshold, my hands shoved in the pockets of my slacks, trying to keep the same stoic expression I nearly always wore. Joshua smiled, pulling his daughter into his side and kissing the top of her head.

"I'm so proud of you," he said, just loud enough I could hear it. She flushed with his compliment and hugged him back.

"You got it! Oh my gosh! You got it!" Meridith hugged Harlowe close, exactly how I wanted to, how I did until my idiocy yesterday. She pulled the bag and looked at the small mementos Harlowe's friends had gotten to symbolize the internship. "You're going to France!"

Harlowe smiled, but it didn't quite touch her eyes. It seemed like I was the only one who noticed. Because I'd been the one to put the melancholy undertone there in the first place? Or because she was my blood mate?

I didn't know. I wasn't entirely sure I wanted to know, honestly.

The rest of the large friend group surrounded them, crowding in until I couldn't see Harlowe at all except the flash of her bright red hair through the mass of limbs. Miles Brown somehow managed to get to her first, pulling her into a hug that she clearly didn't want. I had to swallow the growl that wanted to rip through me.

"What has gotten into you? You're more high-strung than a damn tight rope act." Joshua asked without preamble, crossing the space. "You look like you're preparing to be staked for your crimes."

Yeah, well, it was only a matter of time until the whole situation came out.

I shrugged and shoved my hands in my pockets. Miles touched Harlowe's elbow. Again. He never kept his damn hands off of her. My nails lengthened into claws, and I fisted them to keep from ripping up my slacks. Bloody hell, I needed to get out of here, needed to see literally anything but that wanker of a vampire flirt with Harlowe the entire damn holiday. I turned away from the entire group of them, heading deeper into the cabin.

Joshua followed, a silent wraith behind me.

The moment we were in his office, he closed the door and flipped the lock. When I turned back to him, his arms were crossed and he leaned back against the door, his gaze wary where he observed me.

"She has bites," he said without preamble.

I didn't bother to deny it. It was obvious it had to be me. We were literally stuck here for the last two days.

"You know I won't hold it against you. She's an adult, and you were without other options." His eyes flicked red for a heartbeat. "Stop freaking out that I'm going to stake you over needing to feed."

"That's not the reason," I groused.

He dropped into that deceptively patient quiet, the one he used to lure in the idiots who were barely adults and thought they were above the ethics code of the clan. Idiots like Miles fucking Brown last year.

"It... wasn't just a feeding," I finally admitted.

It took a moment for the words to process.

All at once, the air grew charged with a violent undercurrent. Joshua's eyes flashed bright red as his lips pulled away from his fangs in a lethal, silent snarl. He struck before I could prepare for it. The sound registered before the pain, and then blood was flowing down my face. My eyes watered as I cradled my now-broken nose. Joshua was already pulling back for another strike.

While I believed I deserved every single one, I shot my hand out and grabbed his wrist. Meridith would kill us both if we stained the carpet in here, no matter that it was techni-cally Joshua's preferred study and not hers.

"Bloody hell," I muttered.

Joshua's snarl was unearthly, full of promised violence. I'd harmed his child, and he would kill me for it. He ripped out of my hold and then moved faster than I'd ever seen in our decades of friendship. One moment my nails were sharp-ening into his wrists, tiny drops of blood welling beneath them, and then the next my cheek was pressed against the mahogany wood of his desk, both my arms pinned to the small of my back.

My nose had stopped bleeding, at least.

"Goddamn it, Joshua." I tried to push out of his hold, but his grip only tightened. And then he was digging through one of the desk drawers. I didn't need to see the flash of light wood to know where his thoughts had gone. My stomach clenched as fear tightened my throat. "Give me two seconds to explain."

"You have one," he growled.

"We're Fated."

Just saying it was a relief. She was mine just like I was hers, down to every last unworthy cell within my own body.

He froze, not even breathing. The stake flashed in my vision for a heartbeat, and I tried to prep myself for it, tried to keep the feel of Harlowe wrapped around me—her body draped over mine as she shivered with aftershocks—the last thought that would be in my mind when he did it. I knew when I first tasted her, when I let it escalate to more than just that needed sustenance, Joshua would kill me. But, bloody hell, I needed one more time with her, one more laugh and kiss and knowing look. I needed to be with her when she moved to France.

I needed to tell her I wanted everything with her even if I was the biggest downgrade of her life.

The truth of that settled in my bones. All of the worries, the very real reasons why I shouldn't tie her to me, should allow her to find someone else, fell away. Goddamn it, she was *mine*. Not just her blood, but her body and her soul, too. We matched, and I needed to see her accomplish everything she desired.

"Fated?" Joshua's voice hadn't lost the violent edge. "You're sure?"

I snarled at the implication he thought I would lie about something so sacred to our kind.

"Without a doubt. Fateds aren't something I would ever lie about, and you damn well know it."

"Shit."

His hold on my wrists disappeared. I carefully righted myself, wiping away the worst of the blood from my lips and chin with my already ruined shirt. Joshua eased the stake back into the drawer of the desk. And then, without a word, he pressed against both sides of my nose, setting the cartilage before it could heal crooked.

"That makes three since the last time I've broken yours," I said dryly. "You owe me a couple."

He raised an eyebrow and then flicked the almost-healed bridge of my nose. I hissed in pain.

"You fucked my daughter," he said, anger still threaded through his voice. His eyes flashed red for a heartbeat. "You're lucky it's only a broken nose, jackass."

True.

A tense silence fell between us, the dynamic a horrid tension I despised. It was Joshua who finally broke it.

"So what are your plans? She's moving to France in a little over a month for that internship." He crossed his arms and leaned against the desk, unconcerned with the blood seeping into his pants. "And I will tell you this right now. If you think you're going to convince her to turn down that opportunity and stay here for you, I will use that stake, Fated with my daughter or not. She's worked hard to get this chance."

"Who the hell do you think I am?" Anger lit my veins. He really thought I would make her give up her dreams? It's not like I *needed* my job. I had investments to last entire lifetimes at this point. The job just kept me busy and monetized at least one of my hobbies. "I'll follow her wherever she wants to go. If she'll have me."

"If she'll have you," he said slowly. He pursed his lips and then frowned. "You haven't talked about it?"

"We... I mean, I meant to. She was nervous that you were all getting here. I thought calming her down first would help. I—" I swallowed the word, skipping over me eating her out in the kitchen to get her anxiety under control enough to even attempt a conversation about it.

Joshua's eyes flashed in understanding anyway, that muscle ticking in his neck.

"I don't want to know, Landon."

I groaned and dropped into one of the chairs.

"She heard you guys laughing outside, and all the nerves came back. She asked me a point blank question and I... panicked," I said roughly. "Since then, it's not like there's been a lot of opportunities to have a secluded conversation."

He pursed his lips and crossed his ankles, looking at the ground. His hand picked at the edge of the desk. "You panicked? How bad?"

The memory of Harlowe splayed over the counter, her cheek pressed to the cold stone, her body trembling from the aftershocks of the orgasm I'd wrung from her, filled my mind. Her quiet question, my damning silence. My idiotic retreat.

My stomach twisted.

"Really fucking bad."

There was another long stretch of silence, but it felt

different. This wasn't Joshua's anger brewing. This was him focusing, thinking through all the possibilities of whatever problem he'd been presented. After a while, he sighed.

"You want my opinion?"

I tilted my head back. "You're going to give it regardless."

"Fair." His chuckle was dark. "Look, it's not just because she's my daughter that I'm telling you this, okay?"

I raised an eyebrow and stretched my neck. My throat was starting to burn with renewed thirst, the healing process taking its toll. It hadn't burned at all since the first time I'd tasted Harlowe's strawberry blood. Damn, I'd forgotten what it was like to not have to feed everyday.

"Harlowe's going to need a big gesture," Joshua continued, cutting through my thoughts. "It's just how she is. Being a non-vampire-presenting dhampir is hard in a clan, and her gift doesn't make it any easier."

I growled at that. No, being a reader didn't make her fitting in any easier, but it didn't stop my anger that she lived on the fringes of most groups. Joshua raised an eyebrow, and I forced myself to settle.

"You know her gift now, I assume?" he asked. When I nodded, he sighed. "Right. Look. She doesn't need a stage or anything. But you're going to have to do this with other people in the room if you panicked hard. She'll need the commitment a public gesture insinuates, the feeling that you won't renege later on."

Renege later on.

Fuck, that's exactly what I'd done yesterday. Freaked out, froze, and then didn't give her the same agreement I'd give her the previous night. God, I was shit at relationships.

"All right," I said, agreeing easily. Whatever it took for

her to listen to me after I left her in the kitchen. "Know anyone who could get me the pendant here in time?"

Blood rubies were a bitch to get hold of. This wasn't going to be cheap in the best of circumstances. But Fateds were worth it.

Joshua heaved a long-suffering sigh. "Yes, but you're not allowed to bitch at me about it."

Chapter Fourteen

Landon

The last place I wanted to be on Christmas Eve was begging a werewolf for a damn favor. The memory of Miles Brown flirting with Harlowe galvanized me, though. No way in hell was I leaving this until after the holiday. Who even knew if I'd get a chance to speak with her once we all left this cabin in another week? Her internship began in only a few short weeks, and there was an immense amount of planning still needed to coordinate her move to Europe.

No, this needed to be done today, regardless of who it meant I had to bribe and cajole.

Joshua slid the car to a stop along the curb of the large cabin an hour the other side of the small mountain town. It was domineering, an old-style log design with an enormous deck that wrapped around the entire main floor. Three cars were parked in the long driveway, all of them buried in the snow that had fallen. Footprints littered the snow immediately around the cabin, but none led to the cars. I supposed there wasn't much reason for them to travel into town if they had what they needed for Christmas. A curtain fluttered, and a hand flashed in the window, but no one opened the door.

Joshua didn't move to get out of the car. He stared straight ahead, his eyes unfocused, that worry line between his eyes. His hands flexed on the steering wheel, his claws sharpening and receding at even intervals, almost like they were their own heartbeat in his body.

"Joshua?" I asked, keeping my voice level, neutral.

He sucked on his teeth before sighing. "Just trying to get it in my head that my daughter's about to be offered a mating collar, that's all. She's getting a mating collar and you're leaving for France. You'd planned on being out here for a few decades with us."

I leaned back against the headrest. "I know. I know. I just..."

The corner of his mouth flicked up. "Yeah, I get it. You remember how much of a whirlwind it was with Meridith. And we aren't even Fated."

Christ, theirs had been wildly dramatic. Their entire courtship had lasted only three months. They'd met at a mutual friend's graduation party. Joshua and I had shown up late, buzzed from feeding from a host right before. She'd been crying in the bathroom. It had just... clicked for them. The type of wild love you only ever heard about in romance novels. He'd offered her the mating collar three days before she announced that she was pregnant. That had been over 25 years ago now.

He shook his head and then turned off the car. I eased out onto the unshoveled driveway.

"You're going to end up punching him," Joshua said with resigned understanding.

I scoffed. "No, I won't. I need a favor from him."

Joshua looked at me with a heavy side-eye. "Oh, I know. And when he fulfills it, he'll say something that will piss you off, and you'll end up punching the dumbass. He can't resist goading vampires. You can't resist beating the shit out of werewolves. Just try not to ruin the very expensive mating collar you're about to get, all right? You don't have time for a replacement."

I didn't promise a damn thing as we stepped onto the porch and Joshua knocked on the door three times in rapid succession.

✳ ✳ ✳

Harlowe

Fuck whoever invented popcorn garland. Helping string it was tedious when I was in a decent mood, though I tried not to show my mom just how much it irritated me. It was her favorite holiday tradition, all of us sitting around, chatting about our years while we put together enough garland for the entire twelve foot monstrosity of a tree they put up in the great room every year. Even now, she sat with her legs thrown over Dad's lap, happily chatting with Ferne about the next big coven event happening in the spring.

Today, though, when all I wanted to do was curl up in a ball and never get out of my bed? When my neck still sported both bites from Landon while he'd gone with the vampires looking for blood hosts? I was ready to throw my thread and needle right over the side of the deck, Mom's traditions be damned. Or maybe stab it through Miles Brown's eyeball.

He hadn't opted to go looking for a host with most of the rest of the unattached vampires. No, he'd seen it as the perfect opportunity to bother me. He took a bowl of the freshly made popcorn and wedged himself right between me and Rhiannon, completely ignoring her irritated snarls and the wide open spot on either side of us.

Every brush of our elbows had me wanting to vomit. He seriously gave me the creeps, like a living embodiment of Gaston. How was he still part of the group of guys my brother considered friends? It wasn't like I could ask my brother, though. He'd made the wise decision to go for a blood host before all the humans hunkered down for Christmas tomorrow.

I was only halfway done with my six foot piece when I finally decided I couldn't handle it anymore. Not the popcorn breaking, not the idle chatter, not the way Miles practically breathed down my throat. I dropped the garland into the bowl and eased to my feet. Miles mirrored me, grabbing my elbow.

"Hey, H, what's wrong?" he asked way too loudly.

I was saved from having to come up with a halfway decent response by both the front and deck doors blowing open. The vampires were back. Tessa locked eyes with me, and then she was pushing Miles away from me.

"Back the fuck off, Brown. Now." Her snarl was dangerously low, her body still thrumming from the high of feeding.

Miles pulled back his lips in his own snarl, dropping into a crouch. I eased back from the couch, not wanting to end up in the middle of a vampire fight. They were vicious and brutal at the best of times. I cast around for a place to set my bowl when the last of the group came through the door. Landon stood just inside, his shoulder pressed against the glass. His clothes were rumpled, the simple button-down he'd worn now wrinkled with spots of blood on the collar and sleeves.

He'd... actually found a host.

My heart twisted so fast in my throat, it was a miracle it kept working. Rhiannon came up to me, her gaze jumping between Landon, Miles, and me.

"Let's go for a walk," Rhiannon said, squeezing my hand.

"Here, darling," Dad crooned, suddenly on my other side. I blinked back the sudden rush of tears. Dad didn't know. Dad didn't *need* to know. "I'll finish that piece for you, all right?"

Despite her offer to go for a walk, Rhiannon guided me out of the room and upstairs, shutting the door to the small alcove library and then dropping into one of the overstuffed armchairs. I dropped into the other one, leaned my head back, and cried.

Chapter Fifteen

Harlowe

Christmas morning was bright and happy, the large tree illuminating the entire great room with a warm white light. Everybody laughed and chatted as we opened the gifts we'd given, smiles and squeals and giggles filling the entire cabin with its own warmth.

None of it touched me. None of it reached me in my cocoon of heartsick malaise.

It hadn't been enough for him to reject me, to decide I wasn't the Fated he wanted. No, yesterday he'd been gone most of the day along with most of the single vampires. When the group of them had returned, they were rumpled and relaxed, their clothes carrying the distinct smells of human blood and sex.

My stomach twisted at the thought even now, and I swallowed down the nausea that burned the back of my throat. Tessa wrapped her arm around me as her dad opened the last of the secret santa gifts, sensing the worsening of my mood. Rhiannon eased closer, too, lacing her fingers with mine.

Tessa's dad tilted his head back and laughed as he pulled the gift from the nondescript box, pulling my attention toward him. I didn't want to look. He and Tessa's mom were perched beside my own parents... and Landon. I didn't want to see his face, didn't want to see him smile and laugh like everyone else this morning. Like nothing had changed in his world over the last several days.

Well, I guess it hadn't. It wasn't like he'd claimed me.

"I will get you back, Mark," Tessa's dad said. "I swear to God, I will get you back."

"Looking forward to it," Mark said, holding up his spiked eggnog in salute. "Better hope you draw my name next year."

Tessa's dad turned the sweater around so the rest of the room could see it, and then everyone else was laughing, too, at the cartoon-style drawing someone knitted into the front of the sweater. It was of a traditional Dracula, blood dripping down one side of his mouth as he held a bill of some kind. Underneath, it said "Bah Humbug."

It was easily the ugliest sweater I'd ever seen. It had Mark written all over it. Any other year, I would laugh with the rest of the room. This year, it slid past me, unable to lessen the pall that hung over me.

"That's everything, then!" Mom said, smiling brightly. "Who's ready for some lunch?"

"There's actually one more," Landon said.

I didn't want to look at him, didn't want to see who was getting something from him when I could have nothing at all. It was petulant and immature and at that moment I didn't even care. I dropped my gaze and started picking up some of the forgotten wrapping paper at my feet, reaching behind Rhiannon for one of the trash bags stashed around the room for easier clean up.

"Harlowe." His voice was rich and smooth and washed over me like the last two days hadn't even happened. "I have a gift for you."

Everything stopped. The laughter, the chatter, the indescribable *humming* that was so many preternaturals all sharing something joyous together. I could feel my parents' gazes, my father's hefty concern. Rhiannon and Tessa both froze beside me, shocked and wary. The attention of the room was overbearing.

It took every ounce of willpower to look up at him. I couldn't bear to see his face right now, much less feel the heat of his body. Tessa squeezed my hand in silent support. It was enough that I focused on the vampire standing in front of me. He held a small package wrapped in blue and green tartan, long and rectangular and almost flat. His eyes flashed to red for a heartbeat, but his hand didn't falter. The gift didn't so much as shake where it was held in suspension between us.

My throat dried out, and I swallowed around the sudden lump crowding my mouth.

"Oh."

I inwardly cringed.

Really? That was the best I could do?

My own hand shook as I took the small gift. Nerves settled in my stomach like a stone around a bird's neck keeping it from flying away.

What could he have possibly gotten me?

Rejecting a Fated didn't have any formal ceremony. They were too rare for something like that to even become standard practice. There was nothing he could have gotten me. We barely talked, barely interacted before the snowstorm. He hadn't had my name for the secret santa exchange. Without thinking, I palmed the thick history book Dylan had given me.

"This is yours," he said in that same steady voice. It sent a shiver down my spine despite my best intentions.

Everything moved in slow motion, every heartbeat ringing in my ears and drowning out my own breathing, as I slowly took the package, untied the ribbon and eased the plaid wrapping paper from the nondescript box.

"Oh, was she who you drew this year, Landon?" Miles asked, entirely oblivious to the strange dynamic of the room like always.

"I was," my brother offered.

Confusion filled the room, so thick a knife could cut through it. Or maybe it was just Miles still not understanding I wasn't interested. Tessa leaned closer, trying to see over my shoulder. Rhiannon thrummed on my other side, both of them still convinced something between Landon and me would be possible.

The box opened easily, the top unfolding to reveal red tissue paper. And, nestled in the very center, was a thin jewelry box. The shape was familiar in a passing way, the same way the etched symbol was. It was something I'd seen other people hold, something I'd seen in my mom's jewelry collection.

It was something I never expected to be given. Certainly

not after Landon had left me panting on the kitchen counter as everyone arrived at the cabin.

Rhiannon grabbed my wrist right over the nearly-healed bite Landon gave me when I'd offered my vein. I couldn't help the flash of a grimace.

"Oh crap, sorry!" she said, dropping her hand to my leg.

I traced the symbol on the jewelry box, trying to remember how to breathe, how to exist in my body. It moved enough of the paper that Tessa could see clearly what it was.

She squealed. "Oh shit, is that a…"

She quickly trailed off as she realized she couldn't be the one to say it, that if this was truly what the symbol indicated, it would be the faux pas of the century to say it before I did. Her nails dug into my thigh, too.

That lump in my throat grew larger until I practically choked on the mess of emotions.

My gaze flashed to Landon, not daring to trust what I was seeing.

He hadn't said a word to me since everyone arrived, hadn't said anything after I confronted him and forced him to confess what he truly felt about being Fated. He… he left me bent over the kitchen island, my orgasm barely crested. Not a single flash of jealousy had marred the lines of his face over the last few days. No, it was Tessa who stepped in and made it clear to Miles that his flirting wasn't wanted after he ignored my quiet redirections and cold shoulder.

My flame of hope was gone, and I didn't trust myself to light it again, didn't *want* to light it again for it only to get ruined anew.

Landon's hands were shoved in his slacks, and his shoulders were tight with tension. His eyes were locked on me, flicking between bright red and forest green. He didn't bother to look at the small box in my lap like everyone else. I supposed he didn't need to see what was inside.

"Really?" My whisper cut through the room, more effective than a whip's crack. The small conversations that had restarted stopped, everyone's attention shifting to... to us.

Landon swallowed heavily, his Adam's apple bobbing. He nodded once.

"Yes."

"What is it?" Mom asked.

My gaze flashed to her. She leaned around Dad, her curiosity written across her face. She didn't know? Had Landon not told my dad?

Not daring to breathe, I pulled out the jewelry box, twisting it so the etching caught the light. The silence of the group took on a new, charged edge as the rest of the room saw the single drop of blood falling into an infinity symbol—the mark reserved by clans worldwide to designate a vampire's chosen mate.

Mom's face paled, her gaze cutting to Dad. Dad, who didn't seem surprised, but rather only held a wary worry in the set of his jaw and the subtle bit of fang cutting into his lower lip.

"Joshua..." Mom whispered.

Dad squeezed her hand, his knuckles whitening. A muscle ticked in his jaw, but his shoulders relaxed before he said anything. "I know."

I know.

And suddenly the last twenty-four hours rearranged themselves into a different narrative. My dad and Landon leaving, my dad coming back alone. Had he gone all the way back to the city, to the clan's mansion? He would have had to run the entire way there and back. No, there was no way he had gone to the city for this. So how had he gotten a hold of one?

"This was where you went?" I asked, still not opening the box itself.

His jaw clenched, that muscle ticking in his neck.

"Yes," he said, no louder than a whisper.

"I thought you'd gone for a host," I admitted, tears suddenly lining my lashes. "You came back with everyone else, smelling like blood."

"Yeah, well, the werewolf wanker had it coming to him," he groused, his eyes bright red again. "He was miserably smug over the entire thing. I couldn't let him leave with that damn smirk intact."

"I..." I swallowed down the rising tide of emotions. "I thought you didn't want me."

Devastation flashed across his face, so strong it felt like a punch to my own sternum. Faster than I could track, he was kneeling before me, carefully pulling his hands into mine, spreading my fingers. I thought he was going to hold them, and hope sprang up without my bidding.

And then he set his palm against mine.

His voice flowed into my head, loud and strong and sure.

I've wanted you since I saw you last summer. I spent an entire year miserable with wanting you, knowing I shouldn't. But knowing you're my Fated? There's no possible universe where I could stomach being separated from you.

My breath caught in my throat.

"Unless you don't want me, which is entirely valid. I was

a prick of the highest order." His voice was gruff. His remorse flowed through my gift.

I'm sorry I left you there. You didn't deserve that. I promise to never desert you from now until my last breath, Harlowe.

"All right," I whispered, trying to see his face through my building tears. His eyes were bright green, his beard rougher and longer than when we'd started the week. "Yes, I accept."

He loosed a breath, an invisible weight falling from his shoulders. His hand left mine, carefully picking up the box. The blood red ruby sat in spectacular, lone glory, larger than any pendant I'd ever seen. I pulled my hair to the side, baring my neck, and he fastened it without a misstep. His eyes blazed as the stone nestled into the hollow of my throat.

The room sucked in a collective breath as they realized what stone he had selected. Blood rubies were reserved only for Fated, for true blood mates. I'd never actually seen one in person before. I didn't get a chance to look around the room, though, to see my mom's reaction or Rhiannon's or Tessa's. Because in that moment, Landon cupped my face, tilted my chin up toward him, and then covered my mouth with his. I sank into him, letting my hands rove over his shoulders, his arms. And when my hands settled on his neck, his thought burned through me, brighter than a meteor.

I love you, Harlowe Grant.

Epilogue

Four Years Later

Harlowe

God, I was going to puke. I paced around our Parisian flat, not seeing any of the specialty wallpaper we'd decorated the walls with or the antique furniture it had taken nearly three years to acquire. I couldn't even appreciate the view of the Seine when I finally managed to pause in front of the living room's large windows.

Where was he?

I glanced back at the table, making sure for the hundredth time the small box hadn't suddenly disappeared. Nope, still there. A square box about the size of an apple wrapped in a deep blue paper and white ribbon. My heart flipped, swelling in my throat as Ragnarok jumped up onto the table, his large paw barely missing the present.

"Damn it, Rag, don't!" I hissed, crossing to the table and picking him up.

It wouldn't have mattered so much except he was the least nimble cat I'd ever seen in my life. Apparently it was something most Norwegian Forest cats had in common. He meowed unhappily, twisting in my hold, but the last thing I needed was for him to decide to push that present off the table. It had taken me forever to find one.

"Go find something else to bother right now, okay?" I told him as I set him back on the main floor. He stared at me, his tail flicking. I pointed to the box as if he could actually understand. "Anything but this. Dad will be super irritated with you if you break it, I assure you."

Well, not that Landon knew that yet. But he would be *very* irritated about it once he learned what it was. I glanced at my phone again, tracking the minutes. Just my luck that today would be the day he got hung up talking to someone at the clan meeting.

With a disgruntled meow, Ragnarok slunk into the bedroom.

I grabbed the box off the table, not willing to risk it.

And then I paced again. I let my hand travel over the various pieces of furniture in the living room: the low back settee and the traditional loveseat and the walnut stained sofa table that we used to play all of our records. I paused to look at the large gallery wall I'd slowly been filling out the last six months. Tessa, Rhiannon, my mom and dad. I smiled as I took in each photo. They were all here with us, at least in part. Only a few more weeks until we flew back for Christmas and got to take another picture to add to the wall.

But first, Landon had to get *home*.

Too nervous to sit, I wandered into the study. One wall was entirely books—and not in a cutesy, aesthetic way. They were shoved on the shelves any way they could possibly fit with more on the ground and random books scattered throughout the flat, too. Having two bookworms in the middle of Paris was not for the faint of heart. The other was Landon's collection of miniature ships-in-a-bottle.

I leaned against the threshold, taking it all in, trying to remember how to breathe.

The front door snicked closed, and the telltale click of Landon's dress shoes on the hardwood echoed through the flat. Ragnarok's pattering feet were next, and then his impatient, demanding meows as he reminded Landon he hadn't been given dinner yet.

"Yes, I know." Landon's warm, rough voice filtered through to me. "But you'll have to wait just a bit longer, cat."

I didn't move, not entirely sure I could without puking. My stomach was in such knots, worse than it had been in years. I pressed the small box to my belly, trying to calm my racing heart.

"Fated," Landon murmured against my skin, wrapping his arms around my waist. "What are you doing standing here staring off into nothing?"

God, his accent still made my toes curl.

"Just thinking," I whispered.

He ran his nose up my throat, his fang lightly caressing my skin. I shivered, a bolt of heat shooting straight through me. Landon pressed his smile against my skin.

"You're going to be amazing," he soothed. "Those students will be the luckiest to have you as their teacher."

I relaxed into him, letting him soothe the worry. The one he knew about, at least. In just under a month, I would be starting a new job: working at the same university as Landon.

Even in the same department. I was quietly excited to live out a couple raunchy desk daydreams.

But that wasn't what had my nerves so high-strung today.

I pulled in a deep breath, and he nipped the sensitive dip of my shoulder. My toes curled and my nipples hardened. He pulled my hips back into him, letting me feel exactly how much he wanted me right now.

"Landon," I said in mock affront.

He just laughed against my skin and pressed a kiss where he'd bitten a moment before.

"I have something for you," I whispered before I could lose my courage again.

"Oh?" His hand trailed up the side of my leg, pulling my skirt with it. "Do tell, mate. What have you gotten me that is more important than me tasting my Fated's cunt?"

My cheeks flushed. Good God, he was incorrigible. I held up the small box without twisting out of his arms. I felt his surprise more than I saw it, the loosening of his arms and the quick intake of breath. He took the small box carefully from my hold and then twined our fingers together, palm to palm.

His thoughts flooded me at once.

Is this what I think it is?

My cheeks flushed which was probably answer enough. Still...

"You'll have to open it to find out. No spoilers from me."

He brought me to the living room, arranging us so I sat in his lap, our hands still joined. His hand was steady as he opened the small box. He pulled the small coin from the center of it, and then his shock hit me, filling my mind through our open link.

Harlowe Rhodes, are you joking right now?

I shook my head. "No jokes here. Just me, terrified out of my mind."

He carefully set the coin on the record table, far enough away from the edge to keep Ragnarok from hopefully noticing it. And then he moved faster than I could track, wedging between my legs as he kneeled before me.

"You're pregnant," he said, his voice full of wonder.

When I nodded, he cupped my face and kissed me, all tongue and teeth. And then he was lowering me to the plush cushion of the settee, pushing up my skirt and leaving love bites up my inner thighs. He laced our fingers back together, keeping his thoughts flowing into me even as the first swipe of his tongue had my back arching.

Harlowe Rhodes, I am the luckiest man on this earth. I love you so, so much.

I squeezed his hand and played with the blood red ruby still nestled in the hollow of my throat. "I love you, too, Fated."

Acknowledgments

Thank you, as always, to Daniel. For keeping the kids fed, the house mostly stable, and the family happy every time I find myself on a ridiculously impossible, self-imposed deadline. You're the rockstar of the year.

Thank you to Cassie, my wonderful PA who has weathered the insanity that is my brain and life over the creation of this book. It would not be here without her helping me with so much other chaos!

Thank you to Ande, my best friend. You're amazing, and I am so grateful you're always there for when I need to crash out.

And thank you, of course, to every single reader who picks up my books. I appreciate every single one of you.

About the Author

Jillian has been crafting stories since she was a young teen. She's always had a soft spot for heroines thrown into the deep end without any prior training. And while she, like most of Booktok, loves the dark-haired love interest, she secretly enjoys the blonde, Golden Retriever heroes. Other secret indulgences include the miscommunication trope, surprise or secret babies, and arranged marriages with age gaps.

Jillian enjoys soaking up the sun in Colorado. She can be found most days keeping the children and animals alive. During the summer, she enjoys testing the limits of her memory by seeing how far into July she can remember to water the flowers and veggies in the garden. She spends most of the winter chasing after her snow loving children while silently cursing that she lives somewhere that actually gets cold.

Also by Jillian Rink

Serendipity Omegaverse

Ready or Knot

Beta

Knot Your Business

Worthy or Knot

Amplifier Chronicles

Hidden

Haunted

Creek Falls Omegaverse

Fragile Heart

www.ingramcontent.com/pod-product-compliance
Lightning Source LLC
Chambersburg PA
CBHW020047310726

48970CB00007B/2445